To Emma ♡

I hope you enjoy reading my book! ☺

The Dawn of Eternal Winter

Veronika Sizova

– Veronika Sizova

The Dawn of Eternal Winter

Veronika Sizova

Life Rattle Press

Toronto

The Dawn of Eternal Winter

Published by *Life Rattle Press*,

196 Crawford, Street, Toronto, Ontario M6J 2V6

Library Archives Canada Cataloguing in Publication

The Dawn of Eternal Winter / Veronika Sizova
First Canadian Edition

Life Rattle Press New Writers Series: ISSN 1713 8981

ISBN: 978-1-989861-71-4

Cover design by Kristina Maltseva

Edited by Ola Pokolenczuk

Typeset by Veronika Sizova

Disclaimer

The Dawn of Eternal Winter is a work of fiction.

Any names or characters, businesses or places, events or incidents are fictitious. Any resemblance to actual persons, living or dead, or actual events is purely coincidental.

Author's Note

Do not expect this novel to be a historically or geographically accurate picture of the Russian Empire. *The Dawn of Eternal Winter* is alternate historical fiction—a fantasy, a dream from another universe, a recollection of the past that comes full circle in the present.

Dedication:

To the people of Ukraine

—your bravery amazes me—you are in my thoughts.

To my family in Yekaterinburg

—your love warms my heart in the coldest winters.

To my friends

—you have supported me in the darkest days of 2022.

To E. R. T.

—you inspired me to start writing again.

To the future

—may it be brighter than the past.

Prologue

Nord Express
Near Saint Petersburg, the Russian Empire
January 13, 1905

Margarita Gradova breaks free. The wheels of the ice-bitten train groan in the distance, their metallic squeals softened by the Siberian blizzard. "Ri-ta-Margari-ta-Ri-ta Margari-ta," they sing in tune with the howling waltz of the wind, lulling the young woman to sleep. Yet there can be no sleep and no peace for the survivors of the Capital's demise.

"Saint Petersburg—the city of the dead," Rita whispers, looking back on the haunted landscape she had once called *Home.* In the bleak moonlight, the silver spires appear ghostly and tormented, mirroring the dormant grief in Margarita's dove-grey eyes.

"Rita!" a voice calls from the shadows of the sinking city—

a woman's voice—a soft, motherly cry of the Virgin, reflecting in the stained glass of the ancient cathedrals. The desolate phantom wails and weeps, but Margarita turns away, heading into the lukewarm darkness of the dimly lit train compartment, never to hear it again, never to remember.

"What time is it, Margo?"

A familiar grim smile, like a half-sunken lighthouse amid the storm, gives her something to hold on to—if only for a moment.

"It's midnight, Adeline," Rita mumbles, her lips still frozen from Homeland's bitter farewell kiss—she bites them to hold back the tears. Not yet. Not in the presence of the woman who saved her life.

"Is it, really?" The smile turns into a devilish grin. Anything other than sorrow seems devilish tonight. The traitors left everything behind in the irrevocable darkness of the shipwrecked Empire.

"We made it." Adeline looks at the shabby suitcase at Rita's feet. It contains just enough food, medicine, money, and clothes to survive the heart-wrenching cold until they reach Paris. "But at what cost?"

"There is no cost. I have lost everything—but I am no martyr," Rita says, clenching her fists. Her pale skin reflects the waning crescent, splendid in its indifferent light.

"We left all the martyrs and heroes behind," Adeline says. "We are rats, escaping the sinking ship, and what about it?"

Adeline is as unpredictable as a midsummer storm, Rita thinks, *and as brutal as a sword that does not shy away from beheading its rivals.*

"You should not feel guilty about leaving, Margo." The older woman shuffles the mask of politeness away. Sparks of primeval fire are dancing in her sea-drenched eyes as she wraps her hand around Rita's waist.

"We are so different, and yet—the same," Rita says, tapping the thick hazy glass separating them from the bone-chilling vastness of the snowy steppe.

"What do you mean?"

"You haven't lost anything, and I left my entire life behind. Still, when I look at you, I see a woman who is as lost as me."

"Well," Adeline whispers, "that's because I have lost something, too."

Rita turns to Adeline but looks past her, into the darkness, into the hallway leading to other compartments lined with cold, fear-struck, almost breathless bodies of "rats"—the lucky ones who had heard the call just in time to catch the train—just in time to leave the starving remains of this icy desert.

The last train. The final call.

"Margo!"

Adeline puts the candle on the table between them. Its flame shines in the younger woman's eyes the way sunrise flickers in Arctic waters, never quite penetrating the surface of the primordial ice.

"Tell me everything," Adeline says, grabbing Margarita's hand. "You will have to tell me one day, so tell me now. Spill the poison until it dissolves your heart."

"I will tell you everything, but I have to know—why did you do that? Why did you help me? Why did you take this risk?"

"You would have done the same thing."

"Not for anyone," Margarita says, shaking her head.

"You would have done it for me." Adeline smiles.

The train whistles, carrying them away from the ravenous wasteland, and Margarita begins her story.

Chapter 1:

This is how it starts...

Saint Petersburg—the city of the Dead
1900-1903

My story begins here, at Saint Petersburg's Imperial University (SPIU)—the best in the country. Russians know the Northern Capital as the fairyland where money rivers flow and gold rings line the fingers of the haughty ladies holding the frail hands of their husbands, the way one holds a lit cigarette—firmly, yet carefully enough not to get burned.

I did not choose this place; in a very cliché, unsophisticated way, it chose me. The Trans-Siberian railway carried all my possessions from the suffocating prison of the Ural

Mountains to the northernmost, almost foreign borders, for a literary competition. My gymnasium's principal—Madam Smirnova—called my writing "too quaint" to remain unknown in the comfortable blanket of Yekaterinburg's winters that bury all hopes and dreams in their snowy embrace.

"Gradova," Madam Smirnova said, "win a prize. Show these northerners our province has something to be proud of."

Despite the ambitious plans to build an egalitarian society under the name of our "Great Empire," I heard a lot of "us versus them" and "me versus you"—there was no one to trust and no one to lean on. Infected with the cruel passion of the eternal competition between the contemptuous North and the steel-bound Ural, I won the philological scholarship and received an unforeseen prize—staying at SPIU as a student. I took this chance.

"You are a lucky girl, leaving this shithole of a city at such a young age," Lara told me. I left her, my most loyal friend, in that nightmare all alone. Lara and I wrote each other letters. That's how I learned the news. That's how I kept in touch with what I had to leave behind for some time. I did not know back then that "some time" would turn into "forever."

My family… you can say it is ordinary if you do not know any better. Dad slaves away at the steel factory—the place that had ruined his lungs. Mom is an art teacher by day and an artist by night. For all the desolate scenery that surrounds her, she paints in the brightest colours, turning our home—a gloomy flat with pale walls and low ceilings—into another universe. She demands postcards of the vivid Saint Petersburg cathedrals and the golden statues of Peterhof.

"They help me stay warm," she says in every letter, and I imagine her writing to me in front of an easel, smiling and humming to herself.

I dream of the time we spent together.

"Grigory, do you like this palette?" she asks. Dad never listens—he dozes off while she paints the Summer Garden in the most luscious hues. The purring wind creeps through the cracks in our ancient windows, eating away at the steely-blue paint of the veiny old walls.

I call her an aristocrat—a green-eyed, raven-haired princess Alexandra, somehow left in a desolate place with the evil "stepmother"—a rare nerve disease which results in chronic pain and fatigue—when she deserves to live in a palace by the Mediterranean sea, immersed in beauty and art.

Every evening when Dad comes home, his ushanka hat covered with snowflakes, his grey beard smelling of cigar smoke and cold metal, Mom greets him with kisses and leaves stains of crimson paint on his burning, sunken cheeks.

I look at them with an innocuous jealousy of someone who

knows this kind of love only happens once—and this "once" may as well never happen to me. There is a joy in never expecting anything better for myself—it leaves room for surprises—only I am yet to experience a pleasant one.

"Ritochka," Dad calls me. This nickname makes him smile, even though he knows I detest it. I love his hearty grin all the more because it is so rare—much rarer than sunlight that only touches Yekaterinburg in the brief emerald-painted Siberian summertime.

I am here now, in Saint Petersburg, the city of spires and angels, museums and bakeries, arts and science, serenity and revolution. Away from home's calm, icy cage, I feel free but also suffocated by the North Wind and its vague promises of a better future. I hear the last word whispered by fellow students—young men with fiery eyes and a burning but impotent desire to change the world.

"Future," they say, "will be brighter." "Future," they assert, "is in our hands."

I laugh at them. Changing the world, you say? The adolescents who fail their courses and skip lectures for drinks with their compatriots—will they be our future? And yet, the change is coming.

February 1904

By the last year of my studies, I know what I want to do. At twenty-one, knowledge is the only power worth holding. I assist the philology professors, tutor other students, do research, and prepare lessons of my own, creating a life of perpetual learning. My mind is the only place the brutal force of the law cannot touch—at least, that is what I think when the war begins.

First, they get rid of the "Free News," a newspaper I always grab on my way into the lecture hall. I do it without gratitude, and only when the "Empire's Truth" takes its place do I realize how much courage it takes to publish its liberated, oppositional predecessor. The censure law aims, to quote Milla Belova—the withering lady in charge of the chemistry department—to "protect us from the mass explosion."

December 13, 1904

After lectures, I return to my dishevelled abode on Moyka Street—an old flat with high ceilings (a desperate attempt to balance out the claustrophobic capacities of my family home) that turns into an Arctic desert when the North Wind engulfs its thin, glass windows.

I am about to cross the river when I hear two young women screaming on the other side of the bridge. They are holding posters with only one word—"FREEDOM"—written across them in blue.

I recognize these girls—Dasha Sokolova and Oxana Fedorova—my philology classmates. They do not see me. The policemen get to them before I can wave or scream. I should do something, but I freeze, watching men in black uniforms—we call them "executioners" because of the black masks covering their faces—locking the girls away into the cage-like carriage.

I stand on the bridge, irresolute, mute. The sun goes down, bathing the angels on the cathedral rooftops in its final embrace, and the matte ice of the Moyka River reflects the deep burgundy shade of the sky.

Tomorrow, I will be colder, whispers the Wind.

This is how it starts.

Watching a couple of seagulls landing on the square where the women were standing, I whisper, "What are they doing here? These birds should dwell by the warm, sunlit sea."

My return to the suffocating twilight of the cold Moyka apartment becomes unbearable. I think about going back to Yekaterinburg and my family, yet the word "FREEDOM" rings in my mind like the bells of Saint Isaac's Cathedral.

Deep down, I know that here, in this city, I can have all the freedom my childhood home can never offer. Then, why is it being taken away? What is this force that keeps destroying peace from within? The claws of the imperial eagle clasp tighter around our throats and thoughts. Victims, should they breathe in a little too much air, die "of their own accord" in their homes with no signs of intruders.

Here I go again, manoeuvring the slippery December pavements to get to the end of the street, to the single shimmering light in the upper row of blind, transparent eyes—empty windows watching over me like guardian angels in the winter dusk.

Arkady Ivanovich, a bald concierge at the front desk—one of the lingering shadows left by the vanishing Empire—looks at me through a worn-out monocle and murmurs, "Good night," adding, with a sly, atrocious smile, "to you and your little friend."

I try not to look at him; this man's lusty gaze is the last thing I want on this hostile night.

The elegant, copper-flowered cage of the antique elevator carries me to the third floor. My hands tremble when I open the door—whether from cold, fear, or disgust, I no longer know.

"I thought it was him—finally breaking in to see me naked in the moonlight," my "little friend" laughs.

Sophia is sitting on the windowsill in her white silk

nightgown, dark curls pressed against the thin oriental lace, as if she were a witch prepared to fly out into the starry sky.

"Would that change anything?" I say when the cold, indifferent veil of fatigue clouds her once bright amber eyes. For a moment, she hesitates, and the pause makes me regret my cruelty.

"Well, I wouldn't dream of getting in bed with *him!*" Sophia smiles as if the twelve-hour shift has not tired her.

My lover wraps her arms around me and lets me carry her back to the fireplace. She gets thinner and thinner each day, working as a nurse in a mental asylum—forever haunted by the freezing, narrow hallways, the endless screams of agony, and the crooked scar on her left temple. A wounded soldier threw a glass in a fit of madness because she would not let him touch her.

Sophia has to sit beside these men for hours as they lie in their beds, weak and angry at the world. She gives them medication and reads stories—she helps the killers who began Russia's speedy demise. She serves them so that we can have some bread and meat for dinner.

Women like her help the murderers to save those praying for peace. Our prayers are not enough; our rotten consciousness is not enough—since February, every choice we have made was in the name of safety, not rebellion. If one of us throws herself on the sword of injustice, the other will follow soon enough—so we carry this selfish island of peace through the ocean of calamity.

I asked Sophia to quit. I wished to rebel against the regime, to scream "STOP THE WAR" at the top of my lungs, but seeing friends being thrown into prison, my parents struggling to find medicine for my father's depleting lungs, my beloved getting paler and weaker, I could not do it. They need me here, helping in any small way I can manage. What good will rotting in the Capital's prison do?

We all know the price you pay for a moment of freedom. If only we were less afraid! If only the voices of weak, tired women—for peacemaking was below the dignity of men—if only these voices could result in more than prison sentences, starving children left without mothers, thousands who risked their safety, their future—for what?

I press Sophia closer to my chest. She keeps trembling and shivering. I want to scold her for sitting on the windowsill, watching for me in the numbing darkness. Instead, I ask questions.

"These soldiers… Do you know why they went to war? They could have torn their contracts, protested, deserted, and yet—you see thousands of them with missing limbs, absent minds. Do they have nothing to lose?"

"They are cowards. And they are human, too," Sophia says, and I feel the cold undercurrent of aloofness she accentuates with her deep, husky voice. No wonder even the most hopeless and unfeeling men fall in love with her. Although "lust" would be a much better word for what these fallen creatures feel: even the ones blinded by explosions gaze at her with the desire to devour, destroy, and conquer. It is not even a physical instinct—for those who lost themselves, wanting to possess another is a question of power. This is what I think. Sophia simplifies it by saying, "They are doomed… doomed, wounded beasts, Rita."

Sophia's ice-cold lips trace my collarbones. I rub her back, trying to take the pain away.

"And you still feel sympathy for these beasts?"

"I feel nothing," she says. "If I allowed myself to feel, I would have turned into a living corpse by now, just like them."

There is something irresolute in her voice—something that makes me want to shake her, to wake her up from this slumber. *No—you must feel something! I beg you to feel, to wake up!*

Instead, I resort to the usual conversation that makes it seem we have something to talk about besides the suffering, and yet, everything circles back to the war—its pain and anguish.

Hours and hours of waiting on yesterday's executioners, bringing them water, reading them letters from their families, watching them so they don't cut their own throats in a moment of rage… I would not be able to do it—I would strangle them in their sleep.

"Is it getting busier? They mobilized even more men last month—Lara told me," I say, listening to Sophia's unsteady heartbeat—with each movement of the flames, her body morphs into a different form.

She sighs and turns away from me, leaning closer to the fire, the orange waves of heat dancing on her childlike, parted lips.

"Yes, my dove. More are coming in each day—the flow never stops. Most of them turn into maniacs without a sparkle of feeling left. They are sick—all of them. Many do not have arms and legs. The infection of war consumes their bodies—but this is not why they keep coming. Their minds, Rita! Their minds are rotten. I look into their eyes—paralyzed with fear, anger, and pain—and still, despite their "noble" suffering, I see no soul in the darkness that haunts them. They left their souls far away—in Ukrainian trenches."

She pauses and glides her light, once-tender hands over my face to brush away the pale locks turned copper by the dance of the wandering flames. Sophia's gaze lingers on my lips. She starts crying. I kiss her forehead.

"What's wrong, my angel?"

"This feeling… I cannot describe it, but it makes my skin crawl. They are dead, and they want to take me with them.

Today, one of them tried to grab my hand in agony… despite his blindness, he felt the pulse of a heart beating in the distance. He told me, 'You may be alive now, but I can feel you burning to death and your ashes freezing, mixed with mud and snow.' They fear death, and yet they beg for it, Rita. They do not want my help—they want to see me suffer like them, be in pain like them… I cannot take it any longer."

Sophia sobs softly, almost silently.

These are the kinds of stories she tells me when we sit by the fireplace on the rare evenings she spends at home.

What she describes seems too horrific to be true, but no matter how many times my lips touch her temples, the scar is still there, waiting, beckoning. She cannot quit—not until the war is over, and sometimes—we never say it, but the thought keeps hanging like a sword over our heads—it feels like it never will be.

Sophia moves closer, and our fingers interlock. She seems incredibly small: a dark-haired girl, strong yet fragile, embracing me by the faintly glimmering flames.

"I was watching the streets for you. You were late again, Rita," Sophia says, her sunken cheeks still wet from tears. "You know how I worry when you are late. I saw you walking and thought: here she goes, my dove, always wishing to fly away into the night!"

"And you wish to stay here forever?"

"I would not mind—it's finally warm now that you are here."

I remember how I used to dissolve in her arms, forgetting the world. Every worry disappeared at a single touch of her lips, but not anymore. Now the ghost of absence haunts the joy of her presence. We are living on stolen time. Each night I expect it to be over, only to find her, as one finds a wounded kitten in a frozen street, curled up next to me at dawn.

I can only offer the warmth of my touch. No words, no prayers seem to break through the asylum's spell—that overwhelming fatigue which keeps making her weaker and smaller—the never-ending strain that draws her to the edge of the precipice.

"Quit this dire job," I beg her, and Sophia responds with a sorrowful smile that says what she never utters.

We need money. You are naïve. I have no choice. They will chase me down and kill me for being a traitor. Is that what you want? If you do not serve the regime, you serve nobody.

"Sophia, you can work at the bakery next door—there is a shortage now, and you know that—"

"Well, then the only bread we are going to have will be the scraps that kitchen rats have for dinner. You would not want that," she says.

I feel guilty—guilty that I cannot help, guilty that I have submerged in studies while she suffers at work.

"I will earn the assistant professorship next week—it's twice my scholarship," I say. "We will have enough to feed ourselves, even if you—"

Sophia lets go of my hand.

"You are not telling me what to do, are you? With the smart world of yours, you fly so high above us mortals," she says, the faint scar pulsing above her raised brow. There is no anger in her voice—only sadness—and something much more painful: regret.

"You know very well that none of this is true, Sophia. You know how much I care for you. I would do anything to see you happy," I say.

She smiles but stays silent. I see tears still sparkling like distant northern stars in her wide-opened eyes, too wistful and shrewd for a girl of twenty-five.

"We can always find a way—just the two of us," I whisper.

She buries her head in my lap, too tired to argue, too weak to protest.

I lied. It was no longer just the two of us—there were hundreds, thousands, millions of us, shivering in our homes, scared and lonely even in each other's company, never knowing what tomorrow might bring, never certain that the dawn would come.

And yet, the sun always rises. I cross the bridge to help Professor Uvarova prepare the lectures, and Sophia takes the yellow-red street car to the mental asylum, where she assists Doctor Novikov as he sustains the living corpses of Russian soldiers in the condition of palatable insanity—sane enough to satisfy the mortifying headlines of the regime.

"Forget what I said. I suppose I am just tired," Sophia says.

I know she is lying, too.

She does not want me to forget.

She wants me to remember—to make me even more afraid of losing her—to make me reach out for her in the middle of the night in fear of finding her body breathless, pale, and still like the morning snow. At midnight, the fire goes out, and I take her to bed.

The Eternal Winter has begun.

Chapter 2:
Christmas in the Summer Garden

Where dreaming spirits haunt the mist-cloaked streets…
December 1903

Saint Petersburg's beauty overwhelms me—not in the colourful, overpowering way of a Mediterranean landscape, but in the manner of a burning forest, flaunting its passionate, desperate beauty in its dying moments. Again, I cross the Neva River to reach Vasilyevsky Island.

In the vast icy desert unfolding beneath me, each wave—once moving in tune with the cruise boats—freezes in motion, powdered by fresh-fallen snow. The ice-covered river hides dark, emerald depths—how many souls were lost there, how many treasures forsaken, never to be found again? And when the December moon turns yellow, the women who look at the sparkling snow beneath the bridge can see the motionless ghosts of their lovers, taken away—by hunger, disease, and war—or so the city legend says, trying to convey through its supernatural pagan tapestry why so many widows and childless mothers have started gathering by this bridge—to weep and curse, weep and curse.

Russians say grief is a shared meal, but everyone gets their own spoon—the larger your spoon, the greater your grief. Still, everyone tastes its bitter insides, feels its claws stuck in their bleeding throats, big or small, son or husband, death or prison—we all hurt, and the pain is irrevocable. It is a gift, a treasure, to still feel it—and to know others feel it, too.

I try not to look at the young widows and the weeping women whose children are buried in Ukrainian lands—I feel sadness but also—justice. They should not have gone where they were not invited. They should not have taken the lands that do not belong to them. Then the needle of despair pierces my mind—these men have starved and so, in seeking revenge where it could not be sought, plunged the world into deeper starvation, sorrow, and death.

These are my most recurrent thoughts as I cross the bridge that leads directly to the faculty of philology, overlooking the river, St. Isaac's Cathedral, and the Winter Palace on the opposite embankment.

I imagine these streets, these landmarks, being bombed and burned to ashes. Children scream, bleeding in the empty, freezing streets. Poisonous smoke fills my lungs. I imagine death knocking on my door and the angels on the roofs of cathedrals falling—one by one—all because of one bloodthirsty man sitting on a throne of bones.

These mindless soldiers never thought the bombs would hit their homes, their churches, and their children one day. Instead, these cruel men imagine glory—but what is glory? Can they see it in the sunken eyes of their starving families? Can they hear it in the screams of the shivering, hungry babies dying of a hundred new diseases brought back by men in uniform?

The Empire always had its evil, its misery, but I cannot help remembering the past—the past where love seemed possible, where kindness was met with a smile, where people—however cold they might have seemed—would hug me when I greeted them with tenderness.

I no longer see any of that in the barren landscape withering before my eyes.

And how did it all start? When did we hit the point of no return?

Last December, I met Sophia. I remember that day clearly, the memory of it flickering in my mind like a still, transparent snow globe. It was a week before the New Year's celebration—a fortnight before the Orthodox Christmas.

The new supply of exquisite sweets, chocolate fir trees, glazed angel cakes, marzipan fruit, jelly ornaments, and Saperavi wine has just arrived at the most renowned food hall in Saint Petersburg—Elisseeff Emporium. I am in a Christmas rush, like everyone in mid-December.

Among aristocratic women in fur coats, feathery hats, and silk gloves, I look like a scullery maid—my long hair braided, my grey coat simple and plain, with no fur or lace to adorn it, and only the heavy calfskin purse I press to my heart convinces the sellers this college girl can afford a Christmas treat on her stipend.

Saint Petersburg's upper-class crowds admire Elisseeff Emporium for its holiday spirit. It is difficult to disagree with them when a pianist in a sleek tuxedo and white gloves plays "The Dance of the Sugar Plum Fairy," and waitresses in snow-white aprons give out candy to the lucky children whose parents can afford the luxury of a bountiful celebration. The children of the poor gaze in from the outside longingly, taking the golden light from the hefty chandeliers for a shimmering halo above the old pianist's head.

I buy a dozen almond croissants—freshly baked, with a crust that melts in your mouth and leaves the sweet taste of Christmas almonds on your tongue. There is no better way to celebrate than to savour them by the fire with a cup of hot chocolate and a Christmas story. However, these children have no fireplace to sit by and no books to read.

No matter how wretched my current state is, I have never experienced this endless hunger, this hollow ache for knowledge, and the bitter pain of not having a roof above my head. I have been quite close, but never as forlorn and helpless as these cherubs with bright, hungry eyes.

"Another pack of Eliseeff's special croissants, please, and also..."

The young woman behind the counter glances at me, sparks of excitement waltzing in her dark amber eyes. Her hair, pitch-black, is tied back, with a few strands escaping at the front, covering her temples. Her features appear otherworldly and grotesque. She seems both fragile and steadfast with her high cheekbones and cat-like gaze, like a girl from the Victorian gothic novel I am reading—*Carmilla*. Of course, I immediately forget my order.

"Another dozen croissants, and?" The woman's gaze becomes warm and teasing—the customers behind me start whispering, and I compose myself, diverting my eyes from her with insurmountable effort.

"One bottle of red Saperavi and a box of marzipan chocolates, please," I say with a half-smile, attempting to hide my interest.

"For a loved one?" she asks.

"For myself—and for the Christmas cherubs." I turn around to gaze at the children freezing behind the tall glass windows of the warm, luscious store.

The woman chuckles and wraps my presents.

At home, I find the note she left with the bottle of wine.

Come and see me at the New Year's Fair by the Frozen Fountain in the Summer Garden. I will be there this Saturday at noon.

~ Sophia.

Sophia… Her confidence and gentle yet provocative manners have won me, and I kept the bottle of wine untouched until Saturday.

People were talking then about the impending doom the Russian Empire was going to face—with prices sky-rocketing, the government tightening its claws around our throats with more and more absurd laws, prohibiting gathering in the streets, implying the spread of the new virus was to blame for the distance established between us.

My university friends have begun to shut themselves in

their own worlds. Where we once had a row of invitations to each other's houses and the city ball at Madam Lissova's palace, now was complete silence.

There were rumours Angelica Lissova—the University's generous sponsor—was about to leave for Europe and hesitated to begin the annual preparation for the students' most memorable celebration of the year.

At the time, I thought nothing of the upper classes packing their bags and sailing away to London and Paris—if I could, I would have done so myself. If not for a lifetime, then for a month of scavenging bookshops and libraries, finding every single novel that could help me escape to yet another place—a distant Celtic castle, a mysterious Victorian house, a vampire's cell...

Imagination carried me away, protecting my heart and mind from the reality of living in what would be called the beginning of the end. Of course, I never thought they were leaving the Russian Empire forever because they saw no future here, where the North Wind whispered so softly, where the Cathedrals sang each sunrise the song of a new day, and where the bridges parted each night only to share a long morning kiss.

"No invitations for you, Miss," the bald concierge tells me when I return from the lecture hall on a Friday evening. The wind howls outside, and I anticipate basking in the warmth of a glowing fire, unwrapping another marzipan chocolate, and thinking about tomorrow—thinking about Sophia.

"Thank you, Arkady Ivanovich, but you do not have to remind me of my solitude—it does not bother me," I say.

Arkady bows his head slightly, staring at me, as always, with a poorly hidden disdain. I can see his right eye winking from behind the old-fashioned monocle in an attempt to either charm or frighten me.

"But surely Madam Lissova will host the ball," he says, "and you will need a companion?"

I see a faint smile breaking through his cold expression.

"Do not worry! If that is the case, I will find someone." I sigh in relief when the elevator doors close behind me, and the concierge disappears from sight.

There is a strange anticipation in me this lonely evening. In spite of what I told Arkady, solitude never had such a grim weight on me as it does now when it has become not only isolating—but also unsafe—to be alone.

The windows weep when December's first blizzard strikes them with her icy-gloved hand. I am safe from the winter's rage, from the concierge's filthy smile, and from the burden of high society, but for the first time in my life, I feel a longing for something more—for someone to confide in—not a friend, but someone much closer—someone I can care for, cherish, and adore.

I re-read Lara's letter. Though always brutal, in December, she becomes poetic, writing words I never thought she would have the courage to write.

LARA'S LETTER

December 1903

There is too much love in you, and in the end, it will break you. Don't ask how I know. I never told you, but I was fond of you. I adored you and never said it out loud—because you had to leave. I knew you would not stay for me—you would not stay for anyone... It would be unfair to make you feel guilty about leaving. Now that you left forever, I can finally say it without remorse.

I loved you, Rita.

We felt it but never said a word. This is how most loves end—without even beginning. You feel them, and you let them go—for good—to regret or treasure on lonely evenings with only a glass of red wine to keep you company. I look at the bottle and desperately want to open it and take a sip, thinking how different my life would have been if I had stayed, but the hand of darkness stops me—I should not dream of what never could be.

Lara, my poor Lara, how can I write to you now?

This is the first time I think of it as a tragedy, not my own or Lara's, but the tragedy of people who risk never finding what they are looking for, never being happy, all because of senseless hatred and the cold prison cells awaiting them if they chose to pursue freedom. Women who love other women do not exist in the eyes of the government and society, so for a long time I have believed I was the only one—nature's mistake, unable to accept the fate the world expected of me.

And what about Lara? She weeps in her room among the grey Siberian suburbs, looking at the quick pastel sketch I made for her a long time ago. She will keep it forever—a memory of what never was. Losing me once was enough; admitting her love once was enough. Instantaneous death is always better than slow torture.

Still, I write to her:

You are right, Lara, my dearest friend!

I won't return, but you should know:

when you wanted it, I wanted it, too.

Now, more than ever, I need her as a friend. She will always remain my beacon of hope—a thin thread connecting me to the place I left a year ago. We are equally lost, Lara and I, and our friendship has always been tinged with affection we could not give openly. She disguised this affection with her forced bluntness. I loved her in silence. And here is the thing with silence—it suffocates love.

I remember Lara telling me one night how she adored my dark blonde hair, my translucent eyes, and the way my hands caressed the ruffles on my nightgown when I was anxious.

I remained silent—not because I did not love her but because I could see no future—no future that would make us happy, at least in that city, always covered with heavy steel smog and rotten with prejudice.

One day, it will change, I tell myself. Hatred, denial, and war cannot go on forever. Is there a point in waiting for this day? We only have one life, Lara. One life. I would not be myself if I did not live it to the fullest. I have always been too selfish to stay where I did not belong.

There is too much love in you.

Tomorrow, I will be in the Summer Garden, seeing the raven-haired woman from Eliseeff's Emporium. Tomorrow, I will leave the past behind, no matter how much it haunts me.

"Among the statues, I have found my fate…"

I wish I knew the poet who wrote these words at the gates of the Summer Garden—this ode to the Greek and Roman Goddesses, whose ethereal presence fills its green labyrinths and pathways with the magic of ancient times—where bodies and minds were less obstructed by clothing and prejudice—where women could love other women, and men could embrace other men.

Most visitors would have never guessed the sculptures they so admire portray every "sin" they would have happily persecuted if they had the chance. Not even murder arouses as much disgust in them as love does. This should have been the warning sign—the sudden rise of hatred among the crowds that eagerly devour white crows in the absence of more convenient prey.

In winter, Christmas decorations take the place of flowers and greenery. Where peonies once bloomed, holiday stalls and Saint Petersburg's artisans arrive, allowing the Summer Garden to blossom with colours and laughter even in its coldest season.

These smiling, careless people do not know yet that a year from now, their lives will change forever. What seems like the end of the world today will turn into a light forehead kiss tomorrow—a nostalgia for a simpler, calmer time.

Here I am, waiting by the Frozen Fountain, for a woman whose face was meant to be found in the gothic cathedral, not among the sweet, luscious embroidery of a bright food hall.

Sophia does not arrive at noon, but I do not mind waiting—the cold marble of the fountain, the ladies with their dark parasols protecting them from snow, and the gentlemen selling mulled wine to the visitors—everything bursts with life to an almost sinful extent while nature freezes, preparing for a deafening storm.

An old woman in a mourning dress passes by me, whispering under her breath: "Oh, how I hate December! Blizzard upon blizzard! Dishonesty upon dishonesty! Death, loss, and misery! The North Wind always returns."

Her words turn into a grieving song—she is chanting thoughtlessly to give her ache a form that others can perceive.

This miserable speech reminds me of my mother and her art. She does not wallow in sorrow but turns it into something beautiful—an abundant oasis among barren land, a bird of paradise in the sky full of crows, a beaconing fire in the violent ocean.

Mom has a rare talent for seeing beauty in the darkest hours—a talent that I have always wished for but never acquired. I do not mask sorrow. I do not extract happiness from pain.

My only "talent" is seeing things for what they are—and if someone tries making a desolate street beautiful, I embrace its melancholy. If someone attempts brightening the darkness of a hospital ward, I accept its emptiness, devoid of hope and warmth. I see serenity where others try to find beauty. I see resilience in pain and suffering that others condemn.

There is truth in accepting life for what it is without smoothing its edges. There is truth and love in embracing the most devastating aspects of the world without hiding its brutal reality.

When we are in pain, we do not confess it. We blame the world for the failures of our minds, bodies, and souls. I have learned how futile it is. One must make peace with the pain before letting it go, or else, akin to a hungry serpent, it will tighten itself around its prey and swallow it whole.

December, dishonesty, death, loss, and misery are mere projections, feelings—they can never bring us the relief that we seek by saying them out loud—they are snakes, and we are rats. Would it not be easier to embrace them, to shock them with our openness, than to fight against sorrow, quickening our downfall?

The more I listen to this woman, the more I see myself in her—unable to turn my loneliness, the ache I feel inside, into something palatable—something I can show others and say, "See how endlessly, how beautifully I have suffered!"

I look at her grey, thin hair covered with a brown wool scarf, her sunken yellow cheeks, and pale parted lips. How death touches us, with insolent tenderness, long before our bodies die, and how boldly its kisses shine through our cores, how evident their traces are on our bodies—the marks of withering, of our eventual disappearance into the unknown!

This woman, and many like her, have spent their lives waiting, expecting something better to come along. When I choose to live, they choose to wait, and that alone draws the line between us—the line between beautifying pain and opening up to it, capturing it, and letting it go. If you turn your pain into a bird of paradise, you won't want to part with it, but if you accept it as the fragile, murky creature it is, it will let go by itself, finding another, more susceptible victim.

What pain had to do with this bright December day, with the first snow powdering the ground and children laughing with joy, skating down the icy paths at the back of the garden? Each time I open my heart, I expect the pain to follow. When you let someone in, be prepared to let them go, to untwine the intricate entanglement of your souls when the moment comes. This is what Lara taught me; what leaving home taught me; what many other events will prove again and again—enjoy it while it lasts, and then be strong enough to part with what has nurtured your heart.

I walk along the alley, vibrant with crimson faces, glimmering with the tapestries of foreign merchants who came to the Northern Capital in hopes of turning its cold bleakness into a festive parade. The young, impressionable crowds enjoy dressing in exotic cloth, painted in all the deep, southern colours they never encounter here, among the icy deserts and snowy hills.

Soon, the spicy, alluring scent of mulled wine seduces me into buying two cups: for myself and my soon-to-arrive companion. A band of street musicians plays "Le Cygne" from *The Carnival of the Animals*, and its melody cuts through me like a knife, so out of place in this chattering, lively kaleidoscope of exquisite furs, silk scarfs, living statues, and fire-eaters.

With two cups of the warm drink in my hand, I make my way through the shouting crowd and see Sophia just where I was sitting moments ago—on the edge of the fountain, in a dark-blue cloak powdered by snowflakes, with a black veil covering her face. Her amber eyes shine even brighter through the dark lace pattern, seeming much deeper now, submerged in the cold December light.

"I'm glad you came after all— I have begun to question your intentions… Sophia," this is the first time I call her by name, and it seems like a foreign word—too soft and musical to be a name at all.

"And yet you got me a drink," she says, taking the cup of mulled wine from my outstretched hand, keeping the other hidden in the warmth of her delicate sable fur muff. "A pleasure to meet you—"

"Margarita," I say, watching her eyes as they study my plain winter coat and the white shawl I keep around my shoulders.

"A queen's name," she says with strange softness. "You are a queen that helps the cherubs but has no interest in keeping her own hands warm."

I look down at my crimson wrists—a well-known courtesy of the North Wind.

"Here," Sophia says, passing me her warm muff, "take it—this is an order."

"A woman who I barely know is giving me orders!" I laugh but take it, plunging my hands into the warmth of sable fur—into the warmth her hands left for mine.

"Are you wondering why I left that note?" she asks, and I see her lips quivering like a half-opened flower under her veil.

"I know why," I say, gazing into her eyes, dark with thought.

"Women like us," she says, "we notice the most subtle gestures more acutely than anyone, don't we?"

"I suppose we do. And it was not the first time you were doing it, either: leaving mysterious notes for attractive women, I mean..."

"No, certainly not for the first time," she says, laughing. "But you were the first one who came to meet me."

"I find it hard to believe, Sophia. You see all these ladies, in their furs and fine jewellery coming by, and I am the one you choose to meet."

"The way you looked at me—it was enough. I did not notice or care for the rest. It made me want to get to know you… Rita."

The way she uses the short form of my name so early yet so naturally makes my heart jump. Intoxicated by the carnival music and the bittersweet taste of mulled wine, I cannot find a reason to get mad at this strange woman with the face of the Virgin and the tongue of a temptress.

"We can share it—until we find a warmer spot," I say, letting her right hand slide into the sable muff.

"It's about time you told me your life story, Rita," she says.

"I hope you do not expect me to be a rich heiress who hides the secrets of her dark past behind the plain clothing she wears to Christmas Fairs."

"Certainly not—I prefer simplicity!" Sophia smiles. "I can tell you are as new to this city as I am. We are adventurers with the future in our hands. Do you believe in witchcraft, Rita?"

"After your note, I think I do. I must be under your spell to come here unguarded. You could be a dangerous woman, for all I know."

Sophia chuckles, but her eyes remain cold. "A dangerous woman? Do I look like one?"

"You look like many things, although I cannot guess now—you weren't in mourning last week…"

I see her smiling from behind the veil—a repressed smile of a martyr—a silent yet desperate curve of hidden pleasure briefly touches her lips.

"Father died a month ago leaving me with no relatives and no fortune, but what do the Elisseeffs' merchants care about the sorrows of their waitresses at Christmas time?"

"I am sorry for your loss…"

"Don't be! He was… a violent man," Sophia says, shaking her head. "It's only sorrowful that now I am left to myself—he had been sick for a long time, and I always had someone to care for, someone to come home to—despite his cruel moods, there was a comfort in knowing I had a living soul at my side—but now it is dreadfully silent. Silent and cold."

"And you have… nobody?" I ask. "Not a friend, not a soul to

comfort you?"

"All have left me," she says, and I see her fleeting smile again. "They carried on to a better world, and only a lucky marriage can save me." Sophia wraps her fingers around my wrist. "But don't feel sorry for me—I can tell you have tragedies of your own, far greater, perhaps, than mine."

Words freeze in my throat, but, feeling the warmth of her touch, I say, as if against my will, "My apartment is silent, too… but I am trying to keep it alive. The fireplace is my only friend this winter, and if you would care to join me by the fire one day—"

"Ah, gladly! I miss the feeling of companionship. Still, do tell me, how do you get by? I have been alone for only a month, and it is unbearable already. Forgive me, Rita, but it seems like you are used to a solitary way of life and would never want to change it."

"Why would you think so?"

"You are a singular, self-sufficient young woman," Sophia says, tugging my wrist so we can walk as she thinks of her next words. She stops by a souvenir stall—a large music box with a golden lid captures her gaze. "And I can tell by the way you carry yourself that there is no man in this world who could measure up to your standards."

"My standards? No man can match them, surely!" I laugh.

"and I can say the same thing about you."

Sophia takes the music box and smiles at the bright letters carved into its side: *The Sleeping Beauty.*

"I have always been a dreamer—more than anything else," she says, gazing at the darkening sky. "I can never think of anything without a slight hint of uncertainty. I change—all the time. I'm only twenty-four, but it seems I have lived so many lives—and these lives would have shocked you."

Sophia puts the music box back and turns its handle slightly. A few wandering notes escape from its cold metal core, echoing in the hollow winter air. The dreamy melody waltzes with the wind, disappearing in the darkest chambers of my memory—a distant vision of a girl dancing with her own shadow on a stormy December night.

"This music sounds familiar." I close my eyes, trying to remember where I heard it for the first time.

"Let me get it for you!" Sophia lets go of my hand and reaches for her purse.

"Please, don't! It costs a fortune!" I say, raising my eyebrows.

"A fortune is all I have." She smiles. "Let it be my Christmas gift for you."

The merchant wishes us "Merry Holidays" and puts the gilded music box in a blue Christmas bag with a sewn-on angel levitating among the stars.

"A cherub—how fitting!" Sophia gives me the bag and takes my hand in hers again.

"I wish I were better at resisting your generosity!" I say, blushing. "Still, the shocking stories you promised to tell me—what are they?"

"You mean—my other lives?"

"I am only interested in this one," I whisper, intertwining my fingers with hers. The sable fur hides our gestures from the hungry eyes of idle passersby.

Sophia's eyes sparkle with curiosity. She squeezes my hand. "I must tell you something," she says, "but it will require… a quieter place."

"If we follow down the Moyka embankment, there is a beautiful cafe where Pushkin used to dine, but it will be quite a walk," I say, hesitating to look at her. "My apartment is nearby, too."

"It's settled, then!" Sophia smiles—and, for the first time, I see her not as a Madonna from the Gothic tapestry but as a vibrant young woman whose laughter lights up the entire ballroom.

We walk down the embankment, and the narrow river, half-frozen in its tightly-laced cobblestone gown, reflects the tempestuous sky.

Sophia's face seems warmer and closer in the shadow of the

coming storm. She does not remove the veil, but her features stand out as though the masters of the distant past painted them with their finest brushes. Her cat-like eyes are prying at me when I talk about my family, my studies, and my uncertain future. She is trying to solve me like a puzzle with a missing piece.

"And you, Sophia?" I say, probing the thin ice under my feet. "Will the woman behind the black veil remain a mystery?"

"Oh, I'm hardly a mystery!" Sophia says, curving her lips—an uncertain movement: half a smile, half a grimace of pain.

"Everyone is a mystery until you get to know them." I say, looking at her with hesitation.

"I grew up motherless." She sighs. "Mother died when she gave birth to me. I have turned into my father's misery long before I could become his beloved daughter. Growing up in our country home, surrounded by nature, I found the love I craved in silence, in solitude, in the earth itself."

"Was it enough?"

"Enough?" Sophia looks at me in bewilderment. "Then why do you think I am here, with you?"

Her question pierces the air like a burning match in the melting snow.

"Curiosity," I say finally, watching the snowflakes melting on her veil, "and loneliness."

"Oh, you are a cruel girl, Rita!" Sophia laughs, and her voice trembles.

"Am I wrong?"

She stops and turns to me. Her hand, warm and slender, still rests in mine.

"I am curious about you, yes," she says. "Wouldn't you be curious about a girl who feeds the cherubs?"

"If this is the only reason you—"

"Do you know how many people care about them? How many give them food, offer them shelter?" she cuts me off with brittle anger in her voice. "None! Not a soul! These ladies in furs, these gentlemen in white gloves, their spoiled children—and none of them even look behind the glass windows—no one meets the starving, lonely gazes of children freezing outside. I don't remember people being this unkind, Rita. And when I see kindness in the midst of cold indifference, I am drawn to it like a moth to the flame."

"Do you think I am the flame?" I chuckle.

"I think I want to be near you—that's all."

"It's been a long time since I've been close to someone and held someone's hand like this," I confess, my eyes glued to her shiny black boots, gliding through the falling snow effortlessly, as if she were skating, holding on to my arm for balance.

"Me too," she says, and I feel her fingers brushing against

my wrist again as if provoking me to answer a question she does not dare to ask.

"Ah, here it is!" I feel relieved to see the familiar façade of the Vienna Restaurant and its welcoming warmth radiating through the ornate windows. The storm has already become violent, and when I open the door for Sophia, the first guest to arrive at the restaurant's grand hall is the whirlwind of snowflakes landing in gentle pirouettes on the glistening wooden floor.

Getting ahead of the old host, I remove Sophia's cloak, revealing a long-sleeved black velvet dress underneath.

"First or second?" The arrogant host, Serzh, scans me from head to toe, remembering my rare visits with a hint of scorn. After all, university girls from middle-class families do not tip as much as the silk-stocking upper-class lads.

The first floor is a dining hall with a large mirror wall and chandeliers hanging from the ceiling. This room is meant for all the grand gatherings. You can often hear laughter, champagne flowing, people singing, and waiters paying the guests generous, though rarely well-deserved, compliments. The large windows open into the street. In the summer, this hall becomes a lively terrace with only a thin screen separating the partying guests from the curious passersby.

The first floor of the Vienna Restaurant is a place for those who have a lot to offer and nothing to hide. That's why all the poets and artists immediately head to the staircase towards the second floor instead.

Serzh leers at Sophia's tightly laced gown as if attempting to tear apart the delicate fabric of her collar with his gaze. The host cannot forgive me for taking off her cloak, and when I answer, "Second floor," Serzh dismisses us with a sigh of contempt. Despite his low standing, he deems himself royalty for shaking hands with the Romanovs once in a blue moon.

One of the servers, Pyotr—a tall, young man with curly auburn hair—escorts us up the red-carpeted staircase. Sophia's hand rests in mine when we pass by the portraits of emperors, commanders, writers, poets, and, at the very top—of Pushkin himself.

The famous second floor of the Vienna Restaurant! Most come here in late evenings when the pianist arrives, and the singers—a fashionable duet—bless the audience with their romantic chants.

During the day, a gramophone record plays at the centre of the room, filling it with raspy voices of opera divas, weaving a web of nostalgia that encompasses the mahogany furniture, the gilded portraits on the walls, and the food itself, as if the visitors were being served memories of the bygone era.

Pyotr ushers us to the second-last table by the window.

"According to the famous legend," our waiter starts weaving the ancient tale, "this is the table where Alexander Pushkin had his last supper… or, rather, lunch—before the final duel with D'Anthès."

"Let's hope this isn't our last meal here!" I wink at Sophia.

"I'll make sure you return," Pyotr says, pulling back the chair for my companion.

We are the only visitors on the second floor today, and waiters with black bows and white collars swirl around us with menus, utensils, tablecloths, and champagne glasses.

"Madam Lissova is coming to dinner," Pyotr whispers, "everyone is agitated."

"Of course," I answer with a knowing smile, "and with her own musicians, no doubt?"

"Do you know her?" Sophia says, looking at me as if I had mentioned having lunch with the Empress.

"I am friends with her son, Misha." I nod. "I can introduce you."

Pyotr's expression changes from cold and official to warm and welcoming.

"I will send Madam Lissova a note that you have dined here earlier," he says. "Knyaz Mikhail will be pleased immensely. I'm sure, Miss—"

"Don't bother!" I say, laughing. "Madam Lissova won't be

happy about a provincial girl setting her nets about Misha."

The waiter's face turns red. He glances at me with a nervous smile and vanishes while Sophia chuckles.

"You never told me you were mingling with the upper-classes!" she says.

"Only Misha and I attend Professor Uvarova's Medieval Literature lectures without falling asleep—if that's what you call mingling..."

Pyotr returns with an extensive wine list that Sophia and I decline in favour of lingonberry tea.

"Do you still have the famous Pozharsky cutlets?" I ask. The waiter nods.

"Then make it double! And a cheese plate to go," I say, turning to Sophia. "You wouldn't mind extending this date, would you? I kept the Saperavi."

"You are one sly woman, Rita! Of course, I don't mind."

Pyotr rushes to the kitchen just when another visitor comes in—a short blond man with a weekly "Empire" newspaper in his hand. He takes the nearby table. As he sits down, I notice his lifeless pale-blue eyes studying me.

"Are you alright, Rita? You look frightened." Sophia reaches out and squeezes my hand.

"Frightened? No, I haven't been frightened in a long time, but I don't feel safe here," I say. "It must be the storm."

Pyotr returns with a porcelain tea set. "Our beloved lingonberry tea—it was made for this weather."

The window panes jingle, confirming his words.

"Saint Petersburg hasn't seen a blizzard like this in twenty years," the blue-eyed man says. Pyotr greets him.

"And for you, Monsieur—"

"Novikov. Doctor Novikov."

"Right! Venison dumplings and caviar, as always?"

"As always."

Doctor Novikov surveys Sophia. Just as I try to place where I could remember him from, two white-gloved waiters bring us the main course and simultaneously remove the silver cloches, exposing snow-white plates with steaming cutlets and crimson drops of cranberry sauce.

"Ah, this is magical!" Sophia says. With childlike wonder in her eyes, she smiles at me. I smile back.

We finish the meal in silence. The deafening howls of the North Wind, accompanied by Anastasia Vyaltseva's recording of the fashionable "How Good Those Eyes Are," make it impossible to talk. The mezzo-soprano lingers in my head:

You took my peace away—you have bewitched me.

The blue-eyed stranger glances at us when we leave.

I open the door, and Sophia screams. The wind lifts her veil and forces her down the steps into the street. Laughing and cursing, she grabs my hand, and we run, facing the cruel storm.

"My apartment is across the river!" I say, pointing my hand forward, but the bridge we are about to cross disappears in the ocean of white—the blizzard closes around us.

Sophia's sable muff presses against my chest. My companion rips her veil and lets the wind carry it away.

"Sophia, what are you doing?"

"I wanted to tell you something, remember?" she says, wrapping her hands around my neck.

"I'm listening," I whisper, but the words freeze in my throat when I look at Sophia's lips.

"Come closer."

I hesitate for a moment—long enough to see a glimpse of doubt in her eyes—but the next blast of the raging blizzard pushes me into Sophia's arms.

She kisses me in the falling snow. I don't want to let go.

And yet I have to—the wind becomes stronger. It will carry us away if we don't find shelter in time.

Chapter 3: Heart of the Storm

A diadem of rubies crowns your head,
And silver armour lines your mighty fleet.
December 14, 1904

I wake up by Sophia's side. It has been a year since she offered her veil to the wind and her heart—to me. She fell asleep by my fireplace the day we met, and there she stayed through the December storm, January frost, the declaration of war in February, and the darkness that followed.

For twelve months, our first kiss remained a beacon shining through the fog of memory—a promise of change, a naïve hope that what I felt then, in the heart of the storm, would carry itself through the foggy days of uncertainty and anguish. This

December morning, the beacon glimmering in the distance succumbed to the endless night.

"I am unhappy," my voice trembles when I reach out for Sophia's hand. Her cold fingers linger in the warmth of my touch.

"What do you mean? Unhappy with what?" Sophia rolls over to my side of the bed and faces the rising sun. Her eyes glimmer in the pure gold of the morning light.

"I did not expect life to turn out this way," I say.

"You mean the war? None of us did. You cannot expect something like this. No one is happy—not even HIM."

"It's more than that, Sophia. I cannot recognize myself anymore, and I don't recognize you, either."

"I don't like this conversation," she says, getting up from the bed. "Listen, I will go to my shift now, and you will go give your lecture on modern poetry. We will talk when everything settles." Sophia pauses to fasten the buttons of her white dress—the "asylum uniform."

"Don't you want to leave this place and never return?" I ask, looking for the familiar warmth in her frozen gaze.

"And leave the life we had built—to go where? What for? You scare me, Rita. December brings back a lot of memories, I suppose."

"Last December, we imagined a brighter future," I say.

"In the evening, my dove. We will talk in the evening. I will be late." Sophia grabs her bag and rushes out of the bedroom. She cuts some bread and butter for me before disappearing down the hallway—this is her silent way of saying *I still care.*

My lover forgets only one thing—her diary. It falls out of her bag, opening on yesterday's entry.

I want to run after Sophia and return it, but then I catch a glimpse of something I will never forget—things I wish to unsee. Curiosity, however, is stronger than rationality. Temptation overpowers trust in the mind where doubt has already planted its seeds and uncertainty has spilled its poison.

SOPHIA'S DIARY ENTRY

December 13, 1904

Mornings are the worst. I hate night shifts, but this morning was worse than anything else. I'm glad Dr. Novikov saved me. I was in the room with the soldier #1391, whose brain was severely damaged. He always acted like a child, and I actually liked #1391 the most out of all the patients. This morning, I read Blok's poetry to him ("Verses About the Beautiful Lady" that Rita gave me). #1391 liked it. I asked if he would like some tea. He got up all of a sudden and pushed me against the wall. I did not expect him to force himself on me.

Dr. Novikov heard my screams. He pushed #1391 away from me. The nurse before me forgot to give #1391 tranquillizers. Novikov said, "It's not about you." He told me to write about it. This actually helps. I already write notes about my shifts for Novikov, but not in this much detail. I wonder if this is how Rita feels when she writes her lectures.

Novikov asked me to call him "Nick." He is very kind to me. I told him about Rita's suspicions. She met me at the end of my shift once and turned pale when she saw him. She believes he was the man that spied on us a year ago. I don't remember anyone spying on us.

Nick said that I should be careful with Rita. I should watch her and tell him if these suspicions and delusions persist. He said something about "paranoid schizophrenia." Rita is not like that, but I worry a lot about her. I will tell him everything.

Nick looks at me the way she did. I spend so much time at the asylum, and I am the only girl that has lasted for longer than two months. He said I always make a great impression. Nick has very warm blue eyes. I am grateful he saved me from #1391. He promised to only put me in rooms with paralyzed soldiers from now on.

I must come straight to his office tomorrow. Nick wants to talk to me in private. I suspect he will make me the head nurse soon. I would tell Rita, but nothing makes her happy these days. I cannot even mention what #1391 did to me. Oh, she would make such a scene if she knew! She would beg me to quit again.

I am glad Nick knows everything. It's easy to talk to someone who understands how it really is. When #817 hit me, Rita said he was a "monster" and did not deserve to live. I know she wants to protect me, but it scares me that she could think of such a thing. Novikov says she lacks empathy and even could be…

The entry does not end here, but I cannot turn the page. I leave the diary as I found it—on the floor—to let Sophia decide for herself whether I saw it or not.

Mountains of thoughts cloud my mind. I have to revise the lecture notes on Andrei Bely's *Gold in Azure* but curse Sophia instead.

Her detachment has a name now: Dr. Novikov—"Nick"—the blue-eyed man.

I pack my bag and run—the lecture begins in half an hour.

When I cross the Palace Bridge, an image of Sophia's veil appears before me—an apparition floating above the Neva River in the arctic embrace of the North Wind. I pause to observe it—the veil transforms into a shadow of a passing cloud on the thin river ice.

What Novikov said about me could be true. I cannot tell reality from delusion in a country where war becomes peace.

But how can I feel empathy for those who destroy innocent lives?

When I arrive at the lecture hall, Valentina Uvarova greets me with a nervous smile. Professor's silver-grey hair shines in the dim candlelight, and her dark-green eyes framed with heavy glasses reflect the wisdom of a thousand books.

"Gradova, I have to tell you something!" she says, touching my shoulder with an expression of great secrecy that only a suppressed whisper can resolve. "I want you to meet someone after this lecture—a foreigner! This is a great opportunity for your English lessons. Our guest is unprecedented—but no one must know until tomorrow! You will see…"

"A foreigner? During the war—"

Professor puts her hand over her mouth, and I remember that no one should say the word "war" out loud.

"I thought the Empire's borders closed months ago," I say.

"They have opened for one route. The Nord Express—the train that goes to Paris—but only once a month!" Professor explains. "The tickets cost a fortune, but Madam Lissova has been kind enough to arrange everything. You know how charitable she is—how generous her gifts are to our university!"

"Yes—especially when she wants something."

"This is the time for kindness and respect, Gradova," Professor Uvarova says, frowning at me. "We must be thankful to our benefactors."

I sigh and open Valentina's notes to take attendance. Three students are absent. I call their names out—a vile tradition of shaming idlers that Professor Uvarova encourages—nothing triggers change as much as collective shame, she believes.

"Fedorova?"

"Arrested," the class replies.

"Lissov?"

"Missing"

"Sokolova?"

"Arrested."

Guilt buries its fangs in my heart. I could be one of the brave young protesters, freezing in the dark train compartment on my way to a Siberian prison cell. Instead, I stand here, lecturing three rows of hungry, scared eyes about contemporary poetry—for what?

The Anti-imperialist Movement… Madam Lissova's Ball… Treason… Protests… Death sentence…

"Tsss!" Professor Uvarova calms the anxious whispers echoing through the class.

"Where is Mikhail?" she asks me.

"I am as surprised as you are, Professor. He never misses lectures."

I lied. After receiving my telegram about yesterday's

arrests, the secret leader of the oppositional movement must be plotting something in the comfort of his mother's palace.

"And Sokolova, Fedorova—what exactly happened to them?" Valentina turns to the audience.

"Arrested for treason," a brave voice from the back row clarifies.

"Well, well," Valentina says, "Pray for them, children. Pray for freedom!" Professor touches her forehead, drowning a shadow of remorse in her half-closed eyes.

The lecture hall goes silent.

"Gradova will tell you about contemporary verse today," Valentina announces, stepping down from the podium. She nods, inviting me to speak.

"Poetry can set you free," I begin. "Symbolists know what true freedom feels like—they aren't afraid of different forms, strangeness, and deviation. Instead of controlled lines, they use images, dreams, and half-thoughts that occur only for a moment to disappear forever in the eternal stream of human consciousness."

I do not follow the notes this time. Words come to me like a strong river current. I fall, and I rise. I succumb to the force of knowledge—to the only form of freedom that exists in the land of doom.

An hour passes. The students rise when I finish my lecture.

"To freedom and poetry!" I say.

"To freedom and poetry," they echo and clap.

The applause lasts until Professor Uvarova raises her hand.

"Remember one thing, children. Stay silent."

When everyone leaves, Valentina studies my notes.

"They aren't children anymore, Professor," I say.

"And you did not follow your speech, Gradova."

"I did not."

Professor Uvarova stands still, crossing her arms over her chest. Her eyes pierce me with cold, irrevocable sorrow.

"Be careful. Another faculty member may not be as understanding as me."

"I will be."

"I want to protect you, but it's impossible. Their eyes and ears are everywhere," she says.

I nod and put the lecture notes back into my briefcase. With unexpected fervour, Professor grabs my wrist.

"I blame myself for letting you speak today! You have no idea what you are up against, Gradova! You have no idea. They will find you, do you hear me? No more 'freedom and poetry'—do you understand?"

The floor creaks, and a man's silhouette appears in the doorway.

"Am I interrupting something?"

Dr. Eugene Kholodov, the infamous Physics professor whose lack of manners became a beloved topic of the students' discussions, enters without knocking.

"We were just leaving," I say, trying to stay calm under his teasing gaze.

Professor Uvarova lets go of my wrist and masks her embarrassment with a forced smile.

"It's chilly, Dr. Kholodov—don't forget a scarf next time," she says, pointing at the ice covering his beard.

"I enjoy morning walks in the cold. They keep my mind refreshed and… free." He smirks. "Frost and sunshine! Your beloved Pushkin immortalized this weather for a reason, Professor Uvarova."

"As you wish," Valentina says, exiting the lecture hall with her usual grace, but I notice her fingers trembling when she closes the door.

"Your beloved Pushkin," she hisses, "the nerve!"

"You wanted me to meet a mysterious foreigner," I remind her.

"Ah, yes! Miss Daze! You know, we needed someone to teach English this semester, and she came to us. I mean, we sent her an invitation, Angelica Lissova and I—"

"Miss Daze? Is she—"

"Miss Daze is from London! Can you believe this? Well, she

has moved to Paris to study the arts… I should not talk too much. She will tell you everything herself! You will spend a lot of time together, anyway," Professor Uvarova says, grinning at me.

"A lot of time? Together?"

"I want you to be her guide—to show her Saint Petersburg. Miss Daze arrived just yesterday, but I have already told her so much about you, Gradova: from your new position as my lecture assistant and your passion for languages to your knowledge of English, and, well…"

"Well?"

"I have already appointed you as her translator and personal assistant for the English lectures she will give in the next three weeks."

"Professor!" I say, blushing. "I won't be able to do it. It's a lot of responsibility—I have never met anyone from England. My accent will shock her. How can I agree?"

"Gradova," Valentina says, frowning, "you could have at least pretended to be grateful."

"I am, but—"

"You have no choice. There is no one more qualified for this role than you. It's settled."

I freeze at the prospect of becoming a full-time teaching assistant to a complete stranger, but Valentina grabs my waist and pushes me into a big lecture hall with windows overlooking Saint Isaac's Cathedral.

A tall woman in a beige lace gown stands next to a mahogany bookcase, tracing her long, delicate fingers along the shabby spines of the ancient volumes. Matching the tender touch of a lilac wool shawl draped over her shoulders, a golden comb with a purple orchid holds up the heavy waves of her midnight-brown hair.

Miss Daze turns around and meets my gaze with a hint of curiosity in the warm depth of her dark, deep-set eyes.

"Miss Daze, meet Margarita Gradova, your new assistant!" Valentina announces.

The foreigner takes a few steps toward me and bows her head.

"My pleasure, Miss—"

"Call me Margo," I reply.

"Margo… Valentina has told me a lot about your life in Saint Petersburg," she says with a smile.

"And I barely know anything about you!"

"Oh, I am an open book—ask away!" Miss Daze pulls out the chair from her desk, inviting me to sit down.

"Well, ladies, enjoy yourselves." Professor Uvarova grins at the happy resolution to her cunning plan and leaves me alone with the English woman.

I hesitate before taking a seat. Miss Daze's presence wraps around me like a blanket of fog. Her smile alone could melt the frozen Neva.

"I hope you can forgive my bewilderment," I say, hiding my icy-cold palms in the ruffles of my dress. "Professor Uvarova hasn't told me anything until this morning."

"Valentina wanted to surprise you," Miss Daze says. "She told me how passionate you are about teaching English. I will need an assistant, but I hope to help you, too. Soon, you will give lectures on English literature all by yourself."

A frail-looking maid with a tea tray peers into the lecture hall.

"Ah, Nadia! You are right on time," Miss Daze exclaims and takes the tray from the girl's trembling hands.

"Everyone seems to be afraid of me!" The foreigner laughs when Nadia runs away.

"It's uncommon to have English-speaking visitors here," I say. "When people see your elegant French clothes and impeccable manners, they feel intimidated."

"Do I intimidate *you*?" Miss Daze raises her eyebrows, studying my expression.

"No—not at all!" I reply, hoping that a sudden blush does not betray my feelings.

"Good—I would never want to seem hostile or aloof." Miss

Daze pushes a heap of papers aside and puts the silver tray with a porcelain teapot, two cups, and sliced lemon at the centre of her writing desk.

"Valentina told me you like your tea with lemon." Miss Daze finishes pouring the tea and sits down beside me.

"You really do know everything about me, don't you?" I sigh, looking at her. "I wish I could learn about the nature of your current work at least. These papers, for example: what are they about?"

"You see, I am writing a research paper on John Keats and the way his poetry transformed the Romantic genre," she says. "I will publish it upon my return to Paris."

"I've never heard of John Keats," I admit, expecting her to frown, but when I look up at Miss Daze, she smiles.

"I will give you a volume of his complete works. By the time I'm gone, you will be an expert on Romantic poetry."

"I will read it with pleasure… but how long will you stay, Miss Daze?"

"You can call me Miss D." A cautious smile lingers on her lips.

"Miss D," I whisper, studying the antique ruby signet ring on her pinky finger.

"To answer your question," she says, emptying her teacup, "I won't stay here too long—a month, at most. I have accepted Madam Lissova's invitation with pleasure, and she has already paid for the round trip. The Nord Express is an expensive treat these days," Miss D adds, shaking her head.

"I suspect your journey was challenging."

"Yes, it was quite an adventure—the train had to stop for six hours until the border officers allowed it to pass—they were looking for spies and traitors—anyone who could pose a threat to the Emperor," Miss D says. "I can only imagine what horror your life has been, Margo."

"My life..." I pause, looking into her eyes. "Since February, it's all a blur. Professor Uvarova said you accepted the invitation… but why? Forgive me this question, but I cannot imagine what made you risk coming here during the war."

"Oh, it's simple," Miss D lowers her voice, "Angelica Lissova asked me for a favour—and I could not say no to an old friend. She called this her "final gesture" to the University and Valentina. Women like Angelica are worth any risk."

"Does this final gesture mean she is going to leave soon?"

"Very soon, yes—but let this stay between us."

"It will," I assure her, "but I must ask one last thing: how do you know Madam Lissova, Miss D? You seem to be very close."

"You guessed it right, Margo. Angelica and I were very close, but only for one summer." Miss D glances at me with a shadow of uncertainty. "It's a long story."

"Please, go on—there's nothing I love more than a long story," I say.

"Well..." Miss D leans closer, and the scent of wild violets envelops me like a thin summer veil.

"We met during the World Fair in May of 1889," Miss D says, looking past me. Her eyes glaze over with the fog of memory. "It was my second semester at the Sorbonne. The Eiffel Tower had just been opened to visitors, and I remember people from all around the world coming to see this wondrous creation.

"Angelica was swimming against the tide even then. The Russian Empire had boycotted the Fair, but she and her husband, Dmitry, came to see it anyway. Crowds have a peculiar tendency—they bring people together. As soon as Angelica saw me in the crowd that day, she knew we'd become friends—I reminded her of someone from her past—and when a Russian aristocrat invites you to tea, it's hard to say no.

"I left my home in London to study in France, and she left hers in Saint Petersburg—to see the "real world," as she used to call it. Angelica made France her home for the summer, and I showed her Paris—we went to museums, art galleries, and performances.

"I was eighteen—young, naïve, and perfectly incapable of resisting the charm of a wise, beautiful woman with an angel-like name. In September, she left, but the memories stayed, and we have been corresponding ever since. When Dmitry died, she stopped writing for several years, and then I received this invitation. Now you see why I could not resist."

A sudden realization that Miss D risked everything to see Madam Lissova after all these years pierces my heart. I was not prepared for this sharp pang of jealousy.

Stop this nonsense, Margarita—you don't even know this woman! I tell myself, but when I meet Miss D's warm gaze again, my head spins.

"You look like you need a breath of fresh air," Miss D says, "I told you this story would bore you to death!"

"It's not because of your story." I pause, looking at my ghost-like reflection in the window. "I just realized we only have one month—and I must show you so many places!"

"It's a good thing we start tomorrow then," Miss D replies. "We can go to the Ice Fair on Neva—I hope you enjoy skating as much as asking questions, Margo."

"Trust me, I do," I say, smiling at the thought of seeing her tomorrow. "It was a pleasure meeting you, Miss D." I stand up and prepare to leave.

"Wait!" Miss D takes *The Complete Works of John Keats* from the top shelf of her bookcase. "Tell me how you like it."

Her fingers briefly brush over my hand when she gives me

the book. I flinch at her touch. Blood rushes to my cheeks, and I excuse myself, leaving Miss D without saying "thank you." I cannot even look at her.

I run down the stairs and out the heavy wooden doors. The University Embankment meets me with an icy gust of wind.

Silly, silly Margarita! She thinks you are a fool! I repeat to myself, pressing the book to my chest.

"And here she is, the greatest poet of the twentieth century, lost in thought," a familiar voice addresses me from a distance. A moment later, somebody's strong hands clasp around my waist and lift me in the air.

"Misha, you crazy boy! The pavement is slippery—we are going to fall!" I scream, trying to break free.

"I'm sorry, Rita, I didn't know how else to wake you up—you are my hopeless daydreamer!" Knyaz Mikhail gently lowers me to the ground and gives me a bear hug.

"Are you reading that poetry of yours again?" he says, pointing at the volume of Keats I am trying to hide in my briefcase.

"Yes, it's a gift from the English professor Valentina asked me to meet today."

"It's always your English-pinglish—I wish I could understand it!" Misha sighs.

"Oh, my darling boy!" I examine his unruly auburn hair,

half-shattered glasses, and long emerald-green coat covered in ice and ash. "Where have you been?"

"Kholodov and I are working on the combustion project. You know he has to teach both Chemistry and Physics now that Orlov went to war? Anyway, my silly project is not what I wanted to talk about, Rita…and this is not the right place!"

"Is this about my telegram?"

"Oh yes, and so much more! We must get to your apartment first… I would invite you to the palace, but I don't trust anyone there, and my mother is very agitated these days. An old friend of hers has arrived, or so she tells me. It's always mother and her old friends! Is Sophia home?"

"No," I say, "her shift ends late today."

"Excellent!" Misha grabs my hand and drags me across the Palace Bridge.

"Listen, as much as I love your excitement, young knyaz, your determined silence scares me."

"Determined silence is our motto from now on!" Misha waves his fists in the air.

"I don't understand…"

"The Anti-imperialist Movement has failed," he says. "May the Quiet Resistance begin!"

"Misha!" I shake my head, realizing he is about to make me a part of another grand scheme.

"Let me explain. I know the protests have led us nowhere: we tried to gather in various hiding places; you wrote us speeches, and we went out in the streets and demanded the Emperor's resignation—all for nothing, right? Four hundred young men and women are imprisoned, god knows how many—dead, and you are left feeling guilty because they carried your words in their hearts."

"I wrote a few oppositional poems, Misha, and handed them to you. That was it. I never asked anyone to protest—I knew it was futile even then—"

"And here, my dear, you are mistaken!" Misha says, catching me as I slip on the ice by the Admiralty Fountain. "Damn this weather! Next time, I will whistle for a carriage."

"Misha, you know I will never do something like *that* again." I look up at him with regret.

"If not for my poor eyesight, I'd be buried in the trenches long ago," Misha says through gritted teeth, "and no one would miss me! You have to understand—the responsibility for this invasion is on us, too. I promise I won't risk your life or freedom, but there is something you can do to help everyone realize the vile truth about the war—that our soldiers are killing innocent people."

"Go on," I say, realizing he won't give up.

"Here comes the hard part." Misha takes off his glasses and

pauses on the steps leading to my apartment. We enter through the back door so that Arkady Ivanovich cannot see us.

"Harder than what we've been through?" I say in disbelief.

"We have to get in touch with those who survived on the battlefield," Knyaz Lissov says, "and there aren't many..."

"And how would we do that?"

Misha's dark-grey eyes stare deep into my soul.

"We'll get to them through Sophia."

"You have lost your mind, knyaz!" I flinch at the sudden sting of his words. "Don't you dare take the woman I love away from me."

"Rita, let me in, and I will explain—"

I sigh and open the door, "Welcome to the North Pole!"

"A warm welcome, indeed!" Misha grinds his teeth and rushes into my living room to start the fire.

I sit down by the fireplace next to him and notice that Sophia's diary still lies on the floor. Only yesterday, she rested in my arms by the flames, and I thought that nothing and no one could ever separate us. Now, everything has changed.

"So"—Misha clears his throat—"we are the Quiet Resistance! No more protests, I promise you."

"Then what's the point?"

"My father used to say: true power lies in the knowledge of sharing a common goal," Misha says. "The point of the Quiet

Resistance is finding a person you can share this goal with—someone with similar views, values, and passion for freedom."

"In other words, a revolutionary?" I scoff at him.

"Listen, Rita," Misha whispers, warming his hands by the fire.

"I am always listening," I say, shaking my head. "But I am not going to risk Sophia's safety."

"I am telling you about a network of trusted people, where we connect like a chain—each element is tied to two other elements without the rest of the chain knowing where these elements are."

"Will you ever stop speaking in riddles, Misha? I'm losing my patience."

"Do you know why the Loud Resistance failed?"

I shake my head, and Misha lowers his voice.

"Well, I will tell you why: all of its members knew each other—with enough torture, the tsarists have learned all the protesters' names. The difference with the Quiet Resistance is that each person only knows two others, and the network keeps growing without anyone finding out about it. It's that simple! I trust you; you trust Sophia, and she may get us private interviews with some of the asylum's soldiers. You can deliver that information to me, and I will pass it down the chain of the Quiet Resistance."

"Are you telling me you already have the chain—that someone else is behind this scheme?"

"Yes—there is a chain, and there is someone who will never learn that you and Sophia were ever a part of this, because—" Misha stops when I clench my fists.

"Because we never will be." I say, disgruntled, as I stand up and walk back to the hallway. "You are saying we should find someone we trust. Well, I no longer trust Sophia."

"What are you talking about?" Misha asks, scrambling to follow.

"It's Dr. Novikov. She is in love with him. I have proof." I pick up Sophia's diary, still opened on the pages of yesterday's entry, and give it to Misha.

"For the love of god"—he gapes at me in disbelief—"when did you—"

"It fell out of her bag this morning."

"No—when did you see Novikov for the first time?" Misha looks at me sternly, and I lower my gaze.

"A year ago—at the Vienna Restaurant—your mother was planning to dine there that evening."

"Rita… I remember him. I am sure that Sophia loves you more than you know and wants to protect you… from all of this," Misha says, flipping through the pages.

"If Sophia loved me, she would trust me enough to share

these things," I whisper. "Instead, she talks to Novikov and confides in her diary."

"We can only share so much before it becomes unbearable for the people we love," Misha says, heading to the entrance.

"Where are you going?"

"I need to study Sophia's diary—it has everything we need: the soldiers' confessions, the firsthand truth about the war—everything!" Misha takes his coat and rushes out the door.

"It belongs to Sophia!" I scream, following him. "You cannot take it—you are putting her at risk, and for what—a few confessions?"

"You may not understand this now, but what I'm doing is for the greater good," he says, turning around to look at me. "You don't have to be a part of the Quiet Resistance, but admit it: what you did was no better than what I'm doing now! If you hadn't read it, I'd never find it. Let Sophia think she lost the diary—meanwhile, I will do everything in my power to tell people the truth."

"Wait! You are making a mistake!" I run after him, but Misha escapes by jumping into the nearest carriage.

"Angelica Lissova's Palace!" I hear him say, and two strong piebald stallions whip the snow with their steel horseshoes, carrying Knyaz Lissov away into the heart of the storm.

Chapter 4:
Bloody Sunday

Let myriads of angels guard your spires
Against the pain and suffering of war.
January 9, 1905

Three long weeks have passed since our first meeting, but Miss D still strikes me as an otherworldly creature, set apart from everyone else by an aura of wistfulness. Translating conversations for her has become my second nature, and knowing that she needs my help has saved me from the passive anguish of someone who had lost hope for the future.

Ever since Misha took Sophia's diary, I have not heard a word from him, and my beloved herself has turned into a silent ghost who listens without answering and kisses without feeling. I flee from her embrace into daydreams about Miss D.

Ever since showing her the Ice Fair, I have been taking Miss D to the most charming places in Saint Petersburg.

After lectures, we skate on the Neva River, explore The Passage—the most fashionable store on Nevsky Avenue—and order the famous honey cake and cherry strudels at the "North" bakery.

Sophia does not question my late returns. The only conversations we have concern money, food, and the weather.

On Sunday, four days before Miss D's departure, I promise to show her St. Isaac's Cathedral.

I leave my apartment while Sophia sleeps in the armchair by the fireplace. She has not slept in our bed for two weeks already—saying, "Nick advised me to always be by the fire. It provides mental stability and concentration."

My heart is half-anger and half-despair, but I do not fight.

"Nick must be right. He is a doctor, after all," I say quietly.

Where is the smiling, strong, gentle Sophia with the fire of life burning in her amber eyes—what has become of her?

When I walk out of the apartment building, Arkady Ivanovich stops me.

"You have a visitor!" he sneers.

Misha is waiting at the front door. The embarrassed look in his eyes tells me more than I wish to know.

"Misha!" I rush to hug him but feel Arkady's piercing gaze

and shake knyaz Lissov's hand instead. "I haven't seen you for so long! Are you alright?"

Misha remains silent and pulls me outside to ensure Arkady Ivanovich cannot overhear us. Knyaz reaches for the pocket of his emerald-green coat and gives me a gilded paper with elegant cursive writing.

"An invitation to Madam Lissova's ball?" I jump with joy.

"Two invitations," he corrects me, "for you and Sophia."

"I thought Angelica cancelled it," I say, marvelling at the exquisite patterns adorning the edges of each invitation. "She outdid herself this time!"

"She should have cancelled it, yes." Knyaz frowns, looking over my shoulder. "Mother wants to show off, as always. The truth is… she is leaving soon. This ball is her final goodbye." Misha's voice trembles. "We are leaving, Rita!"

I feel the blood rushing away from my face as he says this.

I cannot lose Misha—not now when I need him the most!

"When?" I ask, blinking back tears.

"On the thirteenth," he says, meeting my gaze with a bitter smile. "This is why I came—to deliver the invitation, and..." Misha cannot go on. I see tears clouding his eyes.

"To say goodbye?"

"To say I'm sorry."

"You don't have to be," I say, putting my hand on his

shoulder. "Sophia does not seem to miss her diary that much, and I am sure it is safe with you."

"Actually, I gave the diary to someone else—someone who knows Novikov," Misha says, shaking his head. "Don't worry! I will return it tomorrow—we are almost done with it. Oh, but I am going to leave you in so much chaos..."

"I don't care what you do with the diary, but promise me it won't affect Sophia," I say, squeezing his shoulders. "I am not sure I can take care of her anymore."

"Rita, I have been a bad friend," Misha cries, reaching for a handkerchief in the pocket of his coat. "I will explain everything to Sophia at the ball. I promise!"

"Listen, Misha: forget the ball!" I brush him off, pretending not to notice his tears. "Miss D should be here any minute—I am going to show her St. Isaac's Cathedral—would you like to join?"

"Miss D?" Misha scratches his head in bewilderment.

"If you hadn't disappeared so abruptly, you would have known that for three weeks now I have been a personal translator and assistant to a charming English woman." I smile, but Misha crosses his arms.

"And why exactly is she here, in Saint Petersburg?" Knyaz says, raising his eyebrows.

"Your mother invited her. Remember the 'old friend' you

told me about? Well, Misha—it's Miss D."

"Ah, *her!*" Misha's eyes widen, and he stares at me in utter shock. "Yes-yes, I remember! They met a few times at the palace for tea and spoke French—so much French that I had to retreat to my room. You know how much I hate that language." Misha ruffles his frizzy hair. "Well, it all makes sense now."

"What makes sense?"

"Mother. The ball. She wants to impress Miss D. You know, she would have never done something like that if a foreign guest wasn't present, and an old friend, too. They laughed so much when I saw them together," Misha says, wiping his foggy glasses. "I haven't heard Angelica laugh since father died."

"I'm sorry, Misha." A needle of pain pierces my heart again at the thought of Miss D and Madam Lissova reminiscing about their Parisian summer.

"That's alright. You know how I feel about his death," Misha says as an ocean of anger floods his grey eyes. "Dmitry died a coward's death! A hero shouldn't go this way. I still remember Angelica's desperate screams when she found him hanging from the chandelier in his studio with windows overlooking the park—for everyone to see! No, my father died like a fool!" Misha clenches his fists. "If he accepted the prison sentence—maybe they would have released him by now! Dmitry chose his pride, not his family." Misha shakes with rage.

"And what would you choose?" I tug at his sleeve, attempting to bring his attention back to reality.

"The truth, as always." Misha stares at me in surprise. Childlike innocence fills his gaze.

"You insult the Emperor once, and it is over for you forever," I remind him. "Dmitry's fate will be yours before you know it."

"And if so, I will accept it with noble bravery, not petty fear," Misha says, shaking his fist at the sky.

"You don't have to finish the battle your father started, young knyaz," I say, taking his hand in mine.

"I will finish it, be sure of that," Misha says, lowering his voice. "The Quiet Resistance has distributed some parts of Sophia's diary to the citizens—people are opening their eyes. The unrest has already started. Soon, you will see… but I won't keep you any longer. Have fun with your English woman, and remember—today is Bloody Sunday." Misha turns on his heels and whistles for a carriage.

"See you at Angelica's ball then!" I smile and wave, but a tidal wave of anger rises in my chest.

Once again, I have become the source of Misha's revolutionary scheme. When he flees to Paris with his mother, and the tsarists trace Sophia's diary back to where it belongs, the threat of imprisonment will enter our lives again, and Sophia won't be able to cope this time.

When Misha leaves, I see a familiar silhouette crossing the Blue Bridge.

Miss D greets me with a long, warm hug. Dressed in a luscious Siberian sable fur coat, she radiates soft, all-encompassing tenderness that brings as much happiness as it does pain with the prospect of her imminent departure.

"Well, Margo, you have teased me with this treat since the beginning of time!" Miss D chuckles. "I have observed the marvellous St. Isaac's Cathedral from our lecture hall each day, and now I will finally be its guest."

"I wanted you to see something fascinating before you leave," I say, smiling, but her joy does not transfer to me. After all the days I spent with her, my attachment to Miss D became a secret I could not keep any longer.

It takes only ten minutes to walk to St. Isaac's from my apartment, and our promenade becomes an adventure of its own. Snow crunches under Miss D's boots, and I smile, watching her teeter on the slope leading to St. Isaac's Square.

At last, Miss D takes my hand in hers.

"Even after three weeks of exploring this city, I struggle for balance. Is it always this way here?" she asks.

"In spring, it gets much worse," I say, "there is danger below and above!"

"Above?"

"Icicles!" I chuckle.

"I suppose that would be a terrible way to die," Miss D says, laughing. "Death by icicle!"

"Keats could write a poem about it." I squeeze her hand as we ascend the cathedral's grand staircase.

"I wish I could read *your* poetry. There is so much I wish I could understand," she says with a deep sigh.

"Write me your Parisian address, and I will send you a poem each day," I say.

"In English?"

"Of course."

"It's settled then!" Miss D lets go of my hand when we pass by the red granite columns and enter the cathedral.

The central dome holds twelve small windows letting the azure sunlight glaze over the paintings adorning its rich interior. Miss D looks up and gasps when she sees five golden chandeliers hanging from the vaulted ceiling. In this sea of pink marble, blue granite, and dark-green malachite, with statues of angels and mosaics of Mary and Jesus covering every inch of the cathedral's walls, it is easy to forget about the bloodshed happening many miles away.

"I know what you are thinking," I tell Miss D, "how can people who see this ode to god in the flesh each day be the same people who support the war? I ask myself this question all the time."

Miss D turns to me. When our eyes meet, I catch a fleeting shadow of pity in her expression, but it turns to serenity faster than I can address it.

"No, my dear," she says, shaking her head. "I think that people who support it are long-lost souls. Those who come here do what they can to bring peace—and, sometimes, everything a person can do is say a prayer."

In exchange for a coin, a nun gives us two candles to light and place in the candelabra alongside the hundreds of other candles already burning.

"I always wonder if these rituals help at all," I say when we approach the votive stand and light our tall, yellow candles.

"The living or the dead?" Miss D asks.

"It's too late to help the dead," I say, watching as she puts her candle next to mine.

"It helps with remorse," Miss D whispers, "people light candles and pray to clear their conscience. Isn't it reassuring to know there is a force far more powerful than you and me?"

"Do you believe in this force?"

"Sometimes, I want to," she says, smiling at me. "Many things cannot be explained otherwise."

I lift my eyes to the ceiling and observe the white dove at the centre of the dome.

"The spirit of freedom," Miss D says, following my gaze, "it's here!"

"Who did you light your candle for?" I tilt my head, watching the flames of our candles swaying in the still air filled with incense and myrrh.

"For someone I care deeply about," she says, and I pause, startled by the golden glow of her eyes in the pale candlelight.

"And I lit a candle for you—for your safe journey home," I whisper.

"Home... Do you think it's a real place, Margo? Do *you* have a home?"

"It is real, but not in the way you and I are real, Miss D," I say. "Home nurtures and completes your heart. I've been searching for it my whole life."

"If only I could take the Virgin Mary with me"—she smiles—"my heart would be complete."

I look at the icon of the Virgin and Child surrounded by angels.

"You know, I could get her for you," I reply, "but we have to wait until dark."

"Margo!" Miss D wags her finger at me.

"Oh, but I'm serious!" I whisper in her ear, "I know a secret passage to the colonnade."

"You seem to know a lot of secrets," Miss D says, looking

deep into my eyes.

"Yes—and if you want to share one with me, we can go to the rooftop and steal Virgin Mary on our way out," I tease her.

"I like the way you think, young woman," Miss D says with sparks dancing in her dark eyes, "but if anyone asks—it was your idea."

"Even if we get in trouble, the view is worth it," I say, trembling with excitement.

Until sunset, we listen to the sublime evening service. The choir of smooth, airy voices sings "The Hymn to the Mother of God." Heavenly music fills the vast space around us and ascends to the top of the dome, ringing with the power and passion of centuries.

"And now that we've heard the angels sing, you force me into committing a crime?" Miss D asks when I lead her to the back door of the cathedral.

"Yes—a three-hundred-steps-long crime," I say, watching her disappear into the dark doorway.

Lit by candles, the staircase takes us up to the gigantic drum of the dome and out onto the colonnade.

"I see now"—Miss D sighs in awe—"that heaven is a place on Earth."

"Heaven is a place on Saint Isaac's rooftop!" I say, smiling at her.

Miss D does not laugh. She looks steadfast and solemn among the bronze statues of angels guarding the cathedral.

"I'm glad you saved this place for one of my last days here," she says, pressing her hands to her chest. "It is magical."

"Well, I have the key to every rooftop in Saint Petersburg, so I can show you plenty more," I say, gazing at the city below us.

"Yes, but this one is special." Miss D takes my hand. An opal ring glimmers on her index finger, reflecting the full moon. "You were right. It's worth the risk."

In its deep winter slumber, Saint Petersburg resembles a distant dream, with clouds of smoke cloaking its roofs and spires. Countless street lamps flicker along its avenues like fireflies escaping into the night.

"Are you ready for the ball?" I ask Miss D. She glances at the Winter Palace.

"Angelica has been kind enough to invite me, but I cannot fathom how she could arrange it." Miss D shrugs. "The last time we saw each other, she promised to send invitations to all close friends… including you."

"I doubt I will go," I confess, "it's a feast in time of plague."

"Oh, you should!" Miss D squeezes my hand and looks at the midnight sky. "Trust me when I say—life only gives us so many chances. Allow yourself to be young. I can tell you think it is all your fault. You imagine this war a collective responsibility and feel its insurmountable weight on your shoulders—but I am telling you, as someone who once felt what you feel—that this, too, shall pass. You will see hope again. I can promise you that. Don't tear yourself apart because of the things you cannot change. Now, people who have the power—let them feel this weight. And they will, in time. They always do."

"Miss D," I say, moving one step closer to her. My throat tightens. "Are you going to the ball because of Madam Lissova? You were *more* than friends, weren't you?"

I comprehend the full weight of my words only when it is too late. Her face turns dark with thought.

"I understand what you mean," Miss D says, recollecting herself. "That summer, in Paris, I wished for something that could not come true. Angelica was much older than me and happily married. Sometimes, it's better to love from afar."

"You are lying!" I say. Pain and anger fill my chest.

"How so?" Miss D frowns, piercing me with her intense, heavy gaze.

"You say it's better to love someone from afar, and yet, when Madam Lissova called for you, you came—across all this distance—to see her," I say, afraid to look at Miss D.

"I came here for many reasons," she says, "one of them being Angelica, yes, and the other—you."

"Me?" I freeze in disbelief.

"Angelica wrote about you in the invitation." Miss D leans closer, and I feel the air moving as she speaks.

"Madam Lissova told you about me?" I take a step back, shaking my head.

"Yes, and she spoke of you with adoration," Miss D continues. "She said her son befriended a brilliant young woman whom she'd like me to meet. Angelica was not the only one fascinated by your talents. Valentina confirmed her words and listed all the qualities that could make you the first English literature professor at the university. I accepted their invitation with the greatest pleasure knowing that I will be useful here—if not for you, I would not have come at all."

Miss D's eyes light up with a fervent passion that I have never seen before.

"I came here with you in mind," she says, lowering her voice. "It's a privilege to be in the presence of someone who is about to change history, and I can help you change it—if you still want to, of course."

I see the full moon shining in her eyes, and my reflection dissolves in its luminous halo.

"Of course I want to!" I say, "I'm glad you came, but you cannot stay, can you?"

"Even when I leave, we can write to each other." She smiles

and takes my hands in hers.

"Have you ever wished you took the risk back then—with Angelica?"

"Yes, but it's in the past." Miss D sighs.

"Then why don't you take it *now*?" I whisper.

Our fingers intertwine, and I look at her lips—pale crimson in the moonlight. Miss D pulls me closer. The soft fur of her sable coat brushes against my cheek, and the heat of her breath lingers on my exposed neck. I close my eyes.

A gunshot splits the night in two.

Startled, Miss D and I look in the direction of the Winter Palace.

Hundreds of people attack the gates of the Emperor's residence, and the guards take them down, one by one. Anguished screams fill the frosty air. The North Wind howls, carrying soot and gunpowder on its deadly wings.

"We must go," Miss D says, dragging me back to the stairs. "It's not safe here."

I take a final look at the midnight panorama—the Winter Palace's terracotta-red façade glistens with blood.

"I will find you a carriage to get home," Miss D reassures me, still holding my hand in hers.

"I will be alright! I need to check on someone first," I say, remembering that I should bring Sophia to Madam Lissova's

Palace tomorrow.

Screams and gunshots still rattle in the distance when Miss D catches her ride.

"You have surprised me tonight," I say, waving her goodbye.

"Ah, many more surprises await you," she answers, blowing me a kiss. "See you at the ball!"

With the invitations still in my bag, I want to meet Sophia at the end of her shift and share the good news—Madam Lissova has invited us to the ball, after all. Sophia may be distant and cold, but I remember the way her eyes used to sparkle whenever I mentioned the Winter Ball.

I walk across Nevsky Avenue and turn south into a shadowy dead end where Nick's asylum for returning soldiers towers above the grey warehouses and drugstores. Its cold brick walls greet me with grim hopelessness that only old medical buildings emanate, absorbing the grievous moods of their inhabitants.

"Sophia is busy talking to Dr. Novikov in his office," the ginger head nurse at the entrance tells me, and so I wait.

At half an hour past the end of Sophia's shift, I grow impatient. When the head nurse rushes to the ladies' room, I walk down the hallway. The subdued screams, howls, and shrieks of the tormented patients fill my head with their heavy resonance. When I reach Dr. Novikov's door, through the mad cacophony of noises, I hear another painfully familiar sound: Sophia's moans. I press my ear to the wall and hear her voice, deepened by passion:

"Nick… my darling, my love!"

"Sophia," a low baritone growls back.

I recoil in disgust.

Once I heard my lover screaming another's name, I thought it would be etched into my mind forever, repeating in an endless loop of anger and despair, but I am no longer in love. I feel no remorse.

Sophia's invitation falls to the floor. I leave the asylum, Dr. Novikov, and my ex-lover behind and never look back.

"It's a busy night for you, young lady," Arkady Ivanovich says, greeting me at the front door of my apartment building.

"Is it?" I shudder at his gaze.

"You've heard about the public unrest, eh?" he says. "Bloodshed is on the horizon, my dear. Pain and death surround us—and your little friend is out in the streets again—in this terrible weather! How do you like it, eh?"

"Arkady Ivanovich, please, get to the point," I say, rolling my eyes.

"There is a package for you—hand-delivered and, may I say, very expensive." The bald concierge scratches his head, waiting for my reaction.

"Where do I sign?"

Arkady hands me the paper, and I leave a signature with an abrupt flourish that makes him grin.

"All yours!" he says, winking at me. "And it is red, too, like the revolution."

A heavy crimson box with bold letters spelling "Maison Worth" lands in my arms. I rush upstairs to see what's inside, undisturbed by Arkady's peering eyes.

I carry the package to my bedroom and bend over the fireplace to start the fire. When the flames grow bright, I open the box and see a heap of rich burgundy velvet, warm to the touch.

It's an evening gown!

I gasp and lift the gift out of the box—its long train brushes against my thighs, and I spin, pressing the gauzy sleeves to my shoulders. The dress fits me like a glove.

At the bottom of the package, I find a short note:

Dear Margo,

You will shine like the dawn at this Winter Ball.

A.D.

It's Miss D's handwriting! My gaze lingers on the initials. After all this time, I never dared to ask her name. I press the note to my lips and revel in the fragrance of Miss D's sultry rose-violet perfume.

It's impossible to sleep. I start the Sleeping Beauty music box on my dressing table—a gift from Sophia—and listen to the familiar melody. The waltz carries my thoughts away from the war, the revolution, Sophia's infidelity, and all my worries.

Shine like the dawn, a gentle voice whispers as I succumb to a restless slumber.

Chapter 5:
Dancing with the Empress

Rejoice, the bygone northernmost Empire,
Built on deception, cruelty, and gore!
January 10

Madam Lissova's Winter Ball greets me with the faint glimmer of crystal-tiered chandeliers, the gentle murmur of dancing couples, and the aureate fizz of champagne. Of all the people in this grandiose palace, my eyes instinctively seek out Miss D. In the bright sea of pastel ruffles, I marvel at her dreamlike figure, lurking in the deep, dark shadows, away from the candlelight and the endless waltzes.

Miss D leans onto a marble mantelpiece at the back of the ballroom. The sequin capelet of her sparkling black gown drapes over her shoulders like the wings of a reclining swan.

A golden hair clip in the shape of an eye with a scintillating emerald at its centre ties her dark locks at the back, leaving two wispy strands to frame the gentle oval of her face.

With a smile, I think how the ruby earrings I bought her this morning would complete Miss D's dazzling ensemble.

Entangled in a philosophical conversation with one of the French professors, Monsieur Laflamme, she dwells far away from the ballroom. The garish lights and empty laughter mean nothing to her, and even Laflamme's theory of the Universe amuses her no more than the dry compliment attempted by Eugene Kholodov.

"Ever so charming, Miss Daze!" The self-proclaimed Physics genius tilts his head, failing to mask his heavy Siberian accent with a wide grin.

"Et voici le diable lui-même," Laflamme hisses and turns his back to the taller, younger opponent. The French professor walks away, cursing "le diable" and "ce monstre sibérien."

"Ever so smooth, my dear Dr. Kholodov?" Miss D says, sipping champagne from her tall glass. "You must be more careful next time: interrupting Monsieur Laflamme is akin to facing a guillotine."

"The only guillotine I fear is the cruelty of your smile," Kholodov says, grinning at her.

I glance at Miss D, expecting her to be offended, yet she can barely contain her laughter.

"And you like cruel women, don't you, Dr. Kholodov?" she sneers.

"Your cruelty would complete my sharp wit," Kholodov says, brushing his beard. "If you want, I can tell you about my own theory of the Universe."

"Well, that's enough!" Miss D says, waving her fan in a dismissive motion as if trying to get rid of a persistent fly.

The pest himself does not take the clue. Dr. Kholodov steps forward, offering his hand to Miss D.

"Shall we dance?"

Miss D raises her eyebrows and grins like an executioner preparing to behead her victim.

She is about to answer Kholodov's risky proposal when I step in. The train of my velvet burgundy dress distracts the speakers with its soft shuffle.

"Miss D!" I curtsy to her and give the disappointed Dr. Kholodov a nod that suggests both politeness and disdain.

"Forgive me for being late!" I pause, noticing Kholodov's evil smirk. "I had matters I needed to attend to, but now your translator is at your service for the night."

"Surely, dancing needs no translation, Gradova?" Kholodov winks at Miss D, but the English professor addresses me with unexpected gentleness as if I weren't late at all.

"I can see that you've put my present to good use," she says, gazing at me.

"This is the most beautiful dress I have ever seen, Miss D—except for yours, of course!"

"Not everyone enjoys the darkness," she says, taking my hand. "But I'm glad that you do—we have to survive the night to see the dawn."

Miss D waves at Angelica, who enters the ballroom in a satin rose-pink gown with a snowflake lace collar. Her regal silver-blonde hair crowned with a golden diadem reflects the flickering candlelight and the diamond radiance of snow outside the tall palace windows.

Madam Lissova approaches us. Miss D and I curtsy to the Queen of the ball, and her gaze lingers on the English professor for what feels like an eternity before she speaks.

"Adeline, Margarita—what a pleasure to see you at my ball!"

Adeline, I think, *Oh, why did I have to hear her name from the lips of the woman she loved, and—maybe—still loves!*

"I hope you can accept the absence of men, except for Laflamme, Kholodov, and Misha," Angelica says, waving her hand at the half-empty ballroom. "The rest have been summoned to participate in the cruel massacre."

"Oh, the invasion!" Miss D says, shaking her head. "How

long will it last, my dear Angelica?"

"Alas, our country shall never see the light of day," Madam Lissova replies, "but I hope this evening will become your ray of hope in the ocean of darkness."

"No need to apologize," Miss D says, taking her hand. "We understand. Besides, I never needed men to enjoy myself." She grins and turns to me. "Margo, I hope you will introduce me to Madam Lissova's son! Unlike his mother, he has no interest in languages, it seems, and so we had to communicate in gestures."

"Oh, it will be my pleasure to introduce you," I say, "Misha is a charming young man."

"Yes—a charming young man who never listens to his mother!" Madam Lissova laughs and waves her fan at us. "Excuse me—I believe Valentina is calling me."

Miss D and I exchange knowing glances when she disappears.

"Misha hasn't been himself for a few weeks now," I say, meeting Miss D's wistful gaze. "Still, Angelica should blame Eugene Kholodov's project—Misha spends all his time working on it."

"Is that so?" Miss D says, glancing at Kholodov, who is still listening to our conversation.

"Knyaz Mikhail is doing a project with you, Dr. Kholodov,

isn't he?" she says with a sly smile. "You have mentioned the name, but it escapes me now—was it something about combustion?" Miss D addresses Eugene but finds him looking away, still recovering from the dance fiasco.

"Mhmmm... combustion... yes, something about combustion," he mumbles, lowering his gaze.

Miss D does not hold back from laughing this time, and I see something I never hoped to witness: Kholodov—this tall, steadfast man—starts blushing as if someone had just spilled a glass of red wine over his stern, bristled cheeks.

"Margo, take me to him," Miss D says, gesturing towards Lissova's only heir, who keeps looking for someone among the kaleidoscope of bow ties and long skirts.

We approach Misha. He sees me and smiles so widely that the entire ballroom lights up with a warm golden glow. Knyaz Lissov has finally replaced the broken glasses. His hair looks much darker and orderly, slicked back and combed in the latest fashion.

"Were you looking for me, Knyaz Lissov?" I curtsy to him.

"Yes, Margarita, my dearest friend!" Misha bows to kiss my hand. "How splendid you look tonight!"

"You look quite dashing yourself!" I say, smiling at him.

Miss D's hand reaches behind my back to adjust the bow that came undone during my rushed walk to the palace, and

Misha's friendly expression changes to surprise.

"I see that you have company!" He frowns, adjusting his glasses.

"Miss Daze wants to talk to you," I say, "so I will be your translator."

"We have tried speaking Latin!" Misha crosses his hands. "But, as you know, one can only say so much in the language of the dead." He slowly turns his gaze to Miss D. "How can I be of service?"

I translate, and Miss D steps forward.

"Knyaz Mikhail, how does it feel to be the son of the University's greatest benefactor?" she asks.

"Oh, it feels magnificent!" Misha nods. "If only my mother's generosity could save my grades. Alas! I have to struggle like everyone else."

Miss D, however, does not attempt to match his humorous tone.

"Eugene and you are working on an important project, it seems. Is this why I haven't seen you at the university all this time?"

Misha's face turns red under Miss D's piercing gaze.

"Dr. Kholodov and I spend a lot of time together—it's true," he says. "I barely see the light of day! Rest assured, Europe will hear about us soon. The nature of our project is a secret, though, and I cannot spare you the details."

"I thought so, Mikhail." Miss D turns around to glance at Kholodov. "Still, you should be careful. We are living in a time of great unrest, and one must choose their friends wisely."

A crease appears between Misha's brows, but Miss D continues.

"Angelica feels lonely without you. Don't you know that? There is only so much time we can spend with our loved ones before it's too late."

"Are you threatening me?" Misha says, clenching his fists.

"Misha! How can you say such things?" I whisper, but Miss D stops me with a wave of her hand.

"Last night," she says, glancing at me, "someone made me realize how important it is to experience love while it lasts." Miss D squeezes my hand, and my cheeks turn crimson. "Your mother has lived a life of suffering and loss, Mikhail," she says calmly, almost as if she were singing a lullaby. "Don't make her lose you, too."

"You are a strange woman, Miss Daze," Misha says, smiling widely, but I notice his left eye twitching. "If Angelica ordered you to deliver this message, tell her it was received. Now, if you could excuse us, Margarita and I have something to discuss."

Misha towers above Miss D with the resolute look of a victor, and she lets go of my hand, leaving us alone.

"What on earth are you doing, Misha?" I ask, looking back at Miss D, who joins Angelica on the other end of the ballroom.

"What on earth is *she* doing?" he says. "I won't let a stranger dictate how to live my life."

"It's always about your life, isn't it, Misha?" I start back, shocked by the rage flaming in his grey eyes.

"I told you I cannot stand my mother's desire to turn her misery into parties, and I cannot talk to someone who is trying to control every step I take!"

"No one is trying to control you," I say, trying to hug him, but it is too late. Knyaz pushes me away and storms out of the ballroom into one of the dark chambers at the end of the hall where servants store their belongings. I run after Misha and find him opening one of the wooden chests in the dimly lit room.

"Where is your lover?" he asks, and I see Sophia's diary in his hand. "I promised to return this to her."

"Misha... I have to tell you something."

He seems to notice the desperation in my voice because the storm behind his eyes grows calm for a moment. We sit down on the dusty chest, and I lean on his shoulder.

"Is it about Sophia and Novikov?" Misha whispers. His intense gaze reflects his suspicions.

"Yes. They are together," I say, trembling. "Yesterday, I went to the asylum and heard Sophia making love to this horrible man."

"I am so deeply sorry!" Misha wraps his arm around my shoulders. "How are you holding up?"

"The truth is," I say, glancing at him with guilt, "I have fallen for someone else, too."

Misha stands up and buries his face in his hands.

"Is it Miss Daze?"

"It's very obvious, isn't it?" I lower my gaze to shield myself from his reaction.

Knyaz Lissov turns around and kneels before me.

"Rita, this isn't right. What are you going to do when she leaves?"

"I will think of something! Please, let me be for now," I beg, and the tears glistening in my eyes make him sigh.

"Fine. Take Sophia's diary, and I won't touch the subject again."

"Thank you," I say, hiding the diary in my purse. "I hated you for putting Sophia in danger, but the Quiet Resistance has turned out to be not so quiet after all. Maybe there's sense in your scheme. I'm sorry I couldn't be a part of it."

"Shhh," Misha whispers, "this is just the beginning."

We enter the ballroom again, and I see Miss D conversing with Madam Lissova.

I take a step toward them, but Misha grabs my hand.

"If you really are my friend," he says, "don't let this foreigner stand between us."

"What do you have against her?"

"My dear, this woman..." He glances at Miss D, disdain once again relighting the fire blazing behind his grey eyes. "She is haughty, controlling, dramatic, and unkind—can't you see that?"

"And you," my voice trembles, "are just jealous!" I free my hand from his firm grip and glide past Misha to Miss D's end of the ballroom.

"Margo!" Miss D hands me a glass of champagne. "You are just in time for Angelica's toast."

With passion, Madam Lissova raises her glass.

"To all the innocent people whose lives fell apart in the senseless war led by our Empire, and to all of you, my trusted friends, who came here to share a final moment of peace with me before my departure to Paris. Professor Uvarova, it is my pleasure to announce that I am selling this palace and donating all the money to Saint Petersburg State University. Despite my faults, I hope you will remember me with kindness."

Professor Uvarova, whose grey gown has made her almost invisible among the fashionable crowd, clasps her hands in awe.

Everyone claps, but Misha's voice rises above the applause, silencing the crowd.

"There is blood in your wine, mother! You care little about the dead—and even less about the living," he shouts.

Madam Lissova turns pale. She takes a step back and whispers something to Miss D.

Miss D shakes her head and watches Misha as he comes closer.

"You cannot cover your guilt with parties and donations!" he sneers. "Instead of doing something, you are making us leave our home, and I hate you for that. You care only about yourself—*your* generosity, *your* safety, and *your* friends. Meanwhile, people die across the border: they die, and you flee!"

Miss D frowns and takes Angelica's hand. Silence envelops the ballroom.

"And you, Rita," Misha says with tears in his eyes, "you have disappointed me most of all."

Knyaz Lissov heads to the exit, and the audience murmurs in grave uncertainty.

I want to follow him, but the swift motion of Madam Lissova's hand stops me.

"Let him be," she whispers with a faint smile.

Eugene Kholodov raises his tenth glass of champagne and blurts out, "May I say something, too?"

"Be my guest," Angelica responds.

The controlled serenity of her voice makes me shiver.

Eugene looks around the room with a solemn smile.

"My younger brother, my dearest Vanya, had returned from the war two months ago," he says, "but I never saw him. I blame Doctor Novikov! Yes, you've heard that right—Doctor Novikov is in charge of the Mental Asylum for Returning Soldiers. Lord bless his soul! Your son is blaming the wrong people, Madam Lissova, and I hope you find the strength to forgive him. To you and to our future!"

Eugene gulps down his champagne and asks one of the servers for another glass.

"Now that the men have finished their speeches," Angelica declares, her face still pale from shock, "why don't we, ladies, have the ballroom all to ourselves? My dear musicians, let's play the white waltz—Tchaikovsky's *Sleeping Beauty* fits the occasion."

When the music begins, Miss D smiles at me.

"I feel as if I had just watched a tragic comedy, even though I did not understand a word," she says.

"Forgive me! I was too stunned to translate," I say, noticing that Eugene follows Misha out of the ballroom.

"That is no issue at all!" Miss D laughs. "Some things, as Dr. Kholodov pointed out earlier, need no translation."

"Misha was very unjust to Madam Lissova," I begin, but Miss D cuts me off, leaning closer so that I can hear her heartbeat amid the loud waltz.

"My dear," she says, "I am sure he regrets his words. Now, may I have this dance?" She takes my hand, and I find it impossible to resist.

"I'm terrible at waltzing," I confess, letting her lead.

In the absence of Eugene and Misha, Professor Uvarova remains the only woman with a male partner—Laflamme's charm melts her heart.

Among twenty women-only couples, Miss D and I do not provoke much interest, and, for a moment, I forget that if not for the circumstances, I would have to dance with a man.

"May I call you Adeline?" I ask—champagne makes me bolder.

Miss D laughs, twirling me around the ballroom.

"Yes, you may!"

"Adeline," I say, trying to catch my breath, "there is so much I would like to tell you, but we don't have enough time."

"We will find the time, Margo—I can promise you that. Would you come to see 'Swan Lake' at Mariinsky tomorrow with me and Madam Lissova? Angelica has assured me she rented the box with the best view for the three of us."

"Is that what you were discussing with her when I left?"

"Precisely—but it was Angelica's idea. She wants to express her gratitude to you—for not abandoning me." Adeline looks at me with tenderness, and I melt into her embrace.

"I would never abandon you, Adeline—you know that."

We soar on the waves of music, and her midnight-black dress blends with my burgundy gown.

In the flickering candlelight of the ballroom, I reminisce about the way her face lit up with wonder when we climbed St Isaac's roof—I had almost kissed her that night...

Adeline's eyes have stolen the moonlight and now reflect it back to me—a silvery flame that enters my heart effortlessly, as if she always had the key to its most clandestine chambers.

I observe the dancers around us. Their airy movements, the light tap of feet on the polished wooden floor, and the occasional laughter—everything blends into one.

My head begins to spin. Vertigo of dance and joy turns into a nightmare with a single blast of the North Wind slamming open the ballroom's tall windows. A blizzard of icy thunder and light puts out the candles, and the music comes to an abrupt halt.

Adeline spins me in tune with the howling wind while the other guests wail in agony. They freeze and, corpse-like, crumble to dust—their flesh disintegrating into sticky, blood-red snow. Joined in a passionate embrace, Sophia and Novikov watch me from the other side of the shattered glass windows.

They die, and you flee, a ghostly voice chants in the back of my mind. *They die, and you flee. They die, and you…*

I gasp, and darkness consumes all.

"Margo, we are almost home," a gentle whisper reaches out to me. I wake up in Adeline's arms as our carriage flounders through the ocean of wind, ice, and snow.

"What happened?" I sense the familiar warmth of her sable fur coat under my cheek.

"We were dancing, and you fainted, my dear. I am taking you back to your apartment."

"What horror! Please, forgive me, Adeline. I must have ruined the ball for you." I lift my heavy head from her lap.

"You should not say sorry—I will be a more attentive dance partner next time." Adeline takes off my white silk gloves and caresses my hand.

"May I?" she asks, the warmth of her dark eyes reflecting in mine as she slowly lifts my hand to her lips.

"Yes..." My heart races when I feel the touch of her lips on my skin.

"I was dancing with the empress tonight," she whispers, gazing deep into my eyes.

"Be careful, or I might faint again." I chuckle, but my voice trembles.

The coachman stops the horses, and Adeline helps me out of the carriage. Still dizzy, I lean on her for support when I hear

Sophia's voice.

"Rita, where have you been?" she screams from above, and I see her dark, curly head in the third-floor window. Tears glisten in Sophia's wide amber eyes.

"You have been missed," Adeline says. "Promise me to take care of yourself, darling, and don't forget about the ballet! I will pick you up for lunch beforehand." She leaves me in the hands of Sophia, who greets Adeline with sombre silence.

When I close the apartment door, Sophia snaps at me.

"Have you lost your mind? Who is this woman? And where did this dress come from?"

"There is a lot I need to tell you, Sophia, but you have to tell me even more."

"I don't understand a thing! You disappear for the evening without saying a word and want *me* to tell you something?" she keeps screaming.

I collapse by the fireplace and watch the flames sway in the rhythm of my racing heart.

"Yesterday, Misha gave me the Winter Ball invitations—for you and me," I say, glancing at Sophia. "I went to the asylum to surprise you—you've been dreaming of the Winter Ball for a year, and I hoped to see you happy. Instead, I heard you calling Dr. Novikov 'my love.' Should I say anything else?"

Sophia turns pale and sinks to the floor next to me.

"I'm sorry… I'm so sorry!" She starts sobbing and cups my face with her frail, gentle hands.

"I'm sorry, too," I say, looking past her into the quivering tongues of fire. "I've read your diary—well, a part of it..." I shuffle through the contents of my purse, looking for her diary, but only find the earrings that I meant to give Adeline.

"Don't bother," Sophia says, grabbing my wrist. "I don't blame you. I should not have had an affair with Nick, but what's done is done. I know you cannot look at me the same way again after what you heard, but can we try—just once more—to make this right?"

I look into Sophia's eyes, welled up with sorrow and tears. She sounds genuine, and it twists my heart to tell her the truth.

"It's too late. I cannot feel what I once felt for you."

"Is it because of that upper-class lady who showed you out of her carriage?" Sophia sneers at me. "You are a fool to believe she would ever fall in love with *you*."

"It does not matter to me," I say, gazing into the fire. "None of this matters. The only thing I want now is peace. She understands me, and that's enough."

"She will ruin your life, and you will come to me begging!" Sophia screams at me through the tears, "but it will be too late for you, because I am moving to Nick's apartment. And yes, I do have the key!"

"Sophia!" I try to stop her, but she pushes me away and leaves in a feverish rush, knocking down the music box from my dressing table on her way out.

The music box opens, and a few feeble metallic notes come out of its core.

It plays the same waltz I danced to with Adeline.

SOPHIA'S SUICIDE LETTER

January 11, 1905

My dove,

I will never forgive myself for what I did to you, and you should not forgive me, either. I see now that you are in love with another, and maybe this is for the best. I could never provide you with the safety and stability you needed to be happy. I know you lied every time you said you did not want anything more. Of course, you want more. You always will.

As for me, I have nothing to lose.

When I left you after our fight and went to Nick, I found him lying on the floor among strange documents, pictures, and schemes. His body was still warm, but he did not show signs of life. I could not stop crying over his corpse.

I think someone killed him that same night—just minutes before I arrived.

The papers I found at his apartment were some horrible, atrocious, unjust accusations. You were right. He was watching us. I mean, he was watching **you**. *I was naïve to think he ever cared for me. Nick just wanted to gather information about you, and I gave it to him, willingly, hoping, at first, that he knew a way to cure your "visions." Then, I told him everything because I was falling for him, for his* *kindness, generosity, and understanding.*

I burned all these papers that called you "the protest's silent engine." When you find this letter, Rita, please burn your poems, too, and tell Misha he is in danger. I saw his name circled in red.

When I destroyed the evidence, my mind was set.

Either way, I would not come out of this alive, so I did not care if I got caught. When I left his apartment, it was early morning, and I could not bear to return to you right away. I spent hours walking up and down Nevsky Avenue, surrounded by people—happy people with all their lives ahead of them—when mine was already over.

Arkady offered me the evening newspaper when I returned, and Nick's death was in the headline. Someone had already described a woman leaving his apartment the night he died. The entire city was searching for me. I know only one thing can resolve this for both of us.

You were already gone when I came here, so I left this letter to help you understand why I took my life. Please, do not blame yourself for anything.

I am not afraid of death because I know that you and I found what we were looking for. I hope this woman takes care of you in ways I never could.

Farewell,

Sophia

Chapter 6:
The Dying Swan

The Winter Palace flaunts its azure gown—
A ballerina on the frozen lake…
January 11

Adeline arrives at noon.

She opens the carriage door, and I climb onto the plush seat next to her. An extravagant updo accentuates her high regal forehead. Adeline beams with serenity and wealth, and her manners reflect a calm certainty that everything will be alright no matter how much money she spends this evening.

"I hope you've had a restful night, Margo."

"Hardly," I say, noticing the subtle creases at the corners of her mouth as if she had been laughing all night. "And you?"

"I went to Angelica—she was worried about your health—and returned to my humble lodging once the sun rose. I told her you would see 'Swan Lake' with us. Now, will you? You look at me as if something had changed."

"There is nothing I anticipate more than my first visit to the Mariinsky," I say, "but tell me—has Knyaz Lissov returned?"

"Mikhail... Angelica did not mention him at all, and I was too preoccupied with your safety to ask about someone who put you at so much risk."

"What risk?" I feel the blood rushing to my face.

Does she know everything?

"Didn't he betray you last night?" Adeline says, raising her eyebrows. "I might not have understood anything Knyaz Lissov said, but I saw how he made you feel—"

"Betrayal... I don't know what Angelica told you. Misha was upset, but he did not betray me," I say through gritted teeth.

"I saw him taking something out of your purse before you walked over to Angelica and me," Adeline whispers.

"Misha?" I say, shaking my head. "No, that cannot be true!"

"I did not have the heart to confront him about it in front of his mother. Now, I regret my silence," she says. "I wasn't sure if what I saw had really happened until Angelica told me how unfair he was to you."

I remember the way Misha grabbed my hand—the violent flames dancing in his eyes scared me even then.

This woman is haughty, controlling, dramatic, and unkind—can't you see that?

It's Misha. He took Sophia's diary, using a hurtful sentiment to distract me. But why? Because he realized I fell for Adeline—the woman who has not earned his trust?

"You look pale." Adeline takes my hand. "I did not want to distress you. Has Misha stolen anything of importance?"

"It was just a book," I say, glancing at her with uncertainty. "It's nothing to cry about. Still, thank you for telling me."

"I wish I could tell you sooner, but I needed to be certain," Adeline says, caressing my wrist.

"Misha is still my friend."

"I understand—but he is not worth your tears and sleepless nights." She squeezes my hand in gentle reproach.

Our carriage glides down Nevsky Avenue. I admire the colourful façades of buildings shrouded in a haze of snow.

"Maybe you're right, Adeline. I've spent too much energy keeping a friend who doesn't appreciate me. But I didn't cry for him. Last night exhausted me—that's all."

"Let me make it up to you," she says, pressing my hand to her chest. "I booked us a table at 'Palkin.' I hope you don't mind—"

"But it is the most expensive restaurant in the city!" I gasp. "Why would you do such a thing?"

"My dear," Adeline says with a cunning smile, "I wanted to please you—and nothing more."

I shudder, imagining myself surrounded by aristocrats. Angelica's ball made me realize that I would never feel like I belonged among them. Adeline is another matter. I feel as if I have known her for a thousand years, as if in those other lives that we are not destined to know, we walked together, hand in hand. Were we lovers? Enemies? Who knows... but when I look into her eyes, I see a reflection of my thoughts, my feelings, and my most secret desires, which I could not share with anyone before.

"You're up in the clouds again," Adeline chides me tenderly, "and we've already arrived."

The coachman stops our carriage at the front entrance to the "Palkin" restaurant, and the familiar atmosphere of exuberant luxury greets us with its gold-splattered embrace.

Walking arm in arm with Adeline, I don't feel the appraisal looks as I did with Sophia. Russia is an incredible place—it loves foreigners more than the Russian people.

"Your table is ready, Miss Daze!" The restaurant's owner bustles about—a clumsy apple-shaped man with magnificent sideburns. "And this must be Margarita? I am glad, very glad to meet you!" The gentleman shakes my hand and leads us to a solitary white-clothed table. Situated by the grand stained-glass window, it overlooks the ever-hurrying Nevsky Avenue flooded with a motley crowd.

"Thank you, Vasily." Adeline smiles as if this gentleman saved her from certain death.

"Unbelievable," I remark with feigned displeasure, "you managed to tell the entirety of Saint Petersburg about me!"

"Do you mind?" Adeline asks with a sly grin.

"Do I have a choice?" I parry.

Even the most pointless conversation with this woman turns into a witty game from which I will never come out victorious. And why should I win?

"You chose me," Adeline whispers, "not right away, but—"

"What do you mean? I don't understand your riddles."

"You understand them perfectly, Margo. You could have gone to the ball with another woman, but you chose… me."

"You think highly of yourself." I blush, remembering that she sent me into Sophia's arms last night.

"Certainly," Adeline says, gazing into my eyes. "And what about you? What do you think of yourself?"

Her bluntness amazes me. I try to answer, but the waiter brings us a bottle of champagne and, holding it with his snow-white gloves, pours hissing gold into our glasses.

"This is the best champagne in Saint Petersburg," he says with a proud smile.

"It's nice to get something you don't expect, especially if you don't have to pay for it," Adeline says, winking at me.

"Everyone goes out of their way to please you," I say as the waiter disappears to serve more important guests at a table hidden by an oriental screen.

"I was here without you, and they didn't pour champagne for me." Adeline holds out her hand, and we clink glasses. "For the spirit of youth and change!" she exclaims.

"Youth and change!" I say, draining my glass. "Do you really think that something is going to change here?"

Adeline gazes at me in undisguised surprise.

"Don't you believe it?" she asks with the genuine interest of a foreigner who believes in the vision of a snow-globe Empire where everything is only a fairy tale.

"Not anymore."

"Don't you want to live in a country where you can express your opinion and scold the authorities?" Adeline knows that no one in this room can understand her speech except for me, but I still look around, expecting to see the executioners approaching our table.

"Don't you know that the gulf between desire and reality is unbridgeable?" I say, looking at her reproachfully, but the eyes of this cynical woman twinkle with amusement.

"The gulf between desire and reality is unbridgeable! This is an excellent toast!" Adeline laughs and sips from her glass as if she drinks the best champagne in the Northern Capital every night.

"You will never understand," I restrain myself from raising my voice, "what it is like to live in perpetual fear, to be afraid of every spoken word, every gesture and touch. You have never been threatened with arrest, and your friends have not been locked up in prisons. How can you talk about 'change' with a smile when people here and on the other side of the border are just trying to survive? We saw the carnage together that night when I brought you to the roof of St. Isaac's Cathedral—do you even remember?"

"I remember." Adeline reaches for my hand, but I startle back.

"What do you call this?" I ask her. "The spirit of youth and change? This is the blood of innocent people, and this tragedy will become much, much worse. You and I rest in this cloyingly luxurious establishment, discussing the fate of the Empire as if the revolution could happen in an instant. You have studied at Sorbonne—you should know that change never happens this way! How much more pain will my country have to endure? And Ukrainians—how much suffering will it take to bring them the peace they deserve?"

Adeline pauses, glass in hand, listening to every word with the precision of an experienced surgeon who stitches up a barely beating heart.

"Please, forgive me." She covers my hand with hers. Her opal ring gleams in the golden light of the midday sun pouring in through the decadent window. "I cannot imagine how you feel, but I want to understand. After all, I, too, lost my home and gave up my parentage in order to lead the life of my dreams. Do you keep in touch with your family? I remember your stories about the Ural Mountains—it's hard when your loved ones are so far away, isn't it?"

The deep concern in her voice seems genuine, but I pull my hand back. Now is not the time for feelings. I don't want Adeline to remember me like this—an unfortunate, frail, abandoned girl. Since the beginning of the war, I have received almost no letters—neither from Lara nor from my parents. Mail is intercepted, and the regime annihilates any mention of the intrusion into Ukraine to maintain the illusion of "peace." Privacy no longer exists—but I doubt Adeline would understand my fears.

"I cannot see the point in corresponding with anyone I love," I say finally, lowering my gaze not to see the warmth of her eyes staring back at me. "My family will not be able to come here because their entire life lies at the gates of Siberia. Even if they wanted to meet me, they know: until the war is over, travel is dangerous. Trust me—I'm not worried. There are far greater sorrows than temporary silence."

"The government has to limit railway traffic during the war," Adeline says, nodding. "And the secrecy of correspondence is almost impossible to maintain. I understand you, and I am very sorry."

She looks into my eyes with such fiery sympathy that I want to cuddle up to her chest and tell her the truth—that I no longer know if I have a home and if my loved ones are alive. In Yekaterinburg—the exile city for war convicts—life turns into an icy prison. Lara's last letter ends with this sentence:

I don't know how much longer I can take it.

I could confess everything to Adeline. Instead, I shake my head. "Let's not talk about it now, on such a solemn day," I say.

She lets go of my hand, and I see the pain in her eyes. Adeline tries to hide it with a greedy sip of champagne.

"Well, Margo... I can talk about anything—'Swan Lake,' for instance."

When the waiter brings us hot appetizers—truffle patties and venison dumplings—Adeline makes amends for her impertinent questions with enthusiastic speeches about ballet.

"Still, why did Madam Lissova invite me?" I ask after

the main course arrives. "After all, this is her last evening in Saint Petersburg with you."

"When we love someone," Adeline says, "we are not afraid to share their company with others."

"I disagree. When you love someone, you want to be alone with them—without anyone else disturbing you."

"Yes, but there are different kinds of love." Adeline looks at me, gauging my reaction. "Angelica and I are just friends and nothing more—after all, so many years have passed!"

"Time… everyone thinks it heals the heart and helps us plunge into the river of oblivion, but it's only a myth—real feelings cannot be forgotten," I say with a sigh that makes her smile.

Involuntarily, I start thinking about Sophia. The waiters circling around our table remind me of the distant December day when my ex-lover and I took shelter from the storm at the Vienna Restaurant.

Where is she now? In bed with Novikov? Is she happy?

"Angelica invited Kholodov, too," Adeline tells me over a sumptuous plate of honey-glazed quail.

"I'm sorry—Kholodov?"

Sophia's last words ring in my ears, and I cannot concentrate—not in this opulent restaurant with grotesque curtains, voluptuous red rugs, and heavy chandeliers. I watch Adeline:

she sips champagne like a foreign queen.

You are a fool to believe she would ever fall in love with you.

"Do you mind?" Adeline asks, wiping her lips with a snow-white napkin. "Eugene defended Madam Lissova at the Winter Ball, after all, when her own son betrayed her."

"I don't mind, Adeline… but I cannot stop thinking about—"

"His advances?" she smirks. "Fear not! Eugene is not a romantic but a snob—given direct access to Angelica, he will only woo her. She translated his speech for me, and I thought: what a terrible thing to have a loved one at that horrible asylum!"

"Did Angelica tell you about Doctor Novikov?" I ask. Adeline pauses before answering.

"Not much. Do you know him?"

"I wish I didn't."

"Margo," Adeline says, taking my hand, "I hoped this luncheon would distract you from all the hardships you've been through. After last night… I feel very protective of you."

Her eyes glisten when she looks at me.

I want to say, "I will be fine," but the words freeze in my throat.

"I know you can protect yourself," she continues, "but I wish I could offer some comfort. I saw the way Mikhail left you yesterday. It was my fault, wasn't it?"

"Not at all, I—"

"I should not have spoken to him," Adeline insists. "Please, forgive me."

My heart hangs heavy in my chest as she says this. I shake my head. "After his words… it's Misha I have to forgive."

"If you have lost a friend in him," Adeline says quietly, "I hope you can find a confidant in me."

"You want me to pour out my soul to you because you're leaving," I say. A bitter smile lingers on my lips.

"Do you think I'm cruel?" Adeline's voice trembles. For a moment, I am convinced she will cry. Instead, she recollects herself when our waiter brings the check.

"I'll take care of it!" Adeline nods.

"Cruel," I say, looking up at her. "No, blame me—I have been cruel. Here you are, spending one of your last evenings in Saint Petersburg in my company, celebrating our time together, and I can talk of nothing but your departure."

I open my purse and put the ruby earrings into Adeline's hand.

"Wear them tonight," I ask her, "and keep them—as a memory of me."

"Margo," she says, gazing at me in disbelief, "this gift must cost a fortune! I cannot take it."

"If it's the last thing I can give you—"

"You have already given me so much!" Adeline smiles at

the gemstones shining in her palm and meets my gaze with tenderness, but a shadow of doubt washes over her face. "You haven't spent all your salary just to show how much you care for me, have you?"

"Of course not," I say, "and what does it matter if I did?"

Concealing her evening gown beneath a dark burgundy cloak, Adeline touches my hand with an expression of gentle concern but does not say a word. We stand up from our seats and walk toward the exit. She stops to try on the earrings and smiles at our reflection in the restaurant hall mirror.

"You are so beautiful," I whisper.

She puts her arm through mine as we walk out into the cold once again.

"Snow, eternal snow!" Madam Lissova greets us at the street corner. Ice adorns her carriage as if she took a trip to the North Pole before arriving here.

"I was looking for my son," she says. "I haven't seen Misha ever since the ball."

"Would you like to cancel our evening plans?" Adeline asks. "We could look for him together."

"Oh, I would not miss Tchaikovsky's masterpiece for the world!" Madam Lissova exclaims, leading Adeline into the carriage. I join them, and the snow-cloaked streets of Saint Petersburg rush past our eyes.

Lissova doesn't seem to miss her son that much.

"Misha will return, surely," she tells us, "by tomorrow—he needs to say goodbye to the city."

"I have never said goodbye to London," Adeline notes, "goodbyes are irrevocable, and don't we all wish—one day—to return?"

"Not me," Madam Lissova replies, "tell no one else, but I am tired of living here, on this corrupted, dying land. I did everything I could to make it better for those who must stay, but I want a better future for my son."

I lower my eyes to the floor. She must have forgotten that I'm staying, too.

Soon, soon—the North Wind whispers—*there will be no pain, no suffering, no death. Nothing. Only snow, emptiness and bliss. Forget your sorrows, Margarita. Remember only me. Only me. In this rebellious land, only I have freedom, only I have the ability to change your life for the better. Listen to me. Listen.*

The wind repeats its lullaby, and our carriage rushes towards the cold sunset. We see people gathering in the streets—hundreds of young men and women, silent but resolute. Some of them wave to us.

"Stop the war!" the crowd starts chanting. "Russia will be free!" Executioners surround them, but we take a turn before I can see what becomes of the protest.

"I am always a bystander," I say, turning away from the carriage window.

"We all are," Adeline replies, "until there is nothing to lose."

Madam Lissova, Adeline, and I arrive at the Imperial Mariinsky Theatre. Eugene Kholodov greets us at the grand entrance, flaunting his opulent three-piece suit.

"Angelica told me about his brother," Adeline says when we come to greet Eugene. "To think that Doctor Novikov tortures these soldiers, and no one cares to check his methods!"

I don't answer. My hatred for the soldiers is as great as my contempt for Novikov.

Madam Lissova greets Kholodov with a polished wave of her silk-gloved hand.

"Is there any news from my son?" she asks in a voice that, along with motherly love, rings with the bitterness of betrayal.

"Nothing," Kholodov says, stroking his beard. "I chased after Misha when he left the ball, but he made it clear that he did not want to see me. He slapped me, see?" With an icy smile, Kholodov points to the red spot near his left cheekbone.

"Oh, that's impossible!" Lissova erupts.

"Your son has gone crazy, or—as you, upper-class people

say—has gone into a fever." Kholodov chuckles. "Don't worry—he will grow out of it."

"I beg your pardon, Eugene—I had no idea Misha could be so aggressive!" Madam Lissova waves her hand again as if trying to catch the thought that had eluded her all this time. "Can you forgive him?"

"What is there to forgive?" Kholodov shakes his head. "This is youth, fire, and passion! Do you agree, Miss Daze?"

With a sigh, I translate his words to Adeline. She frowns at him.

"Every youth is different, Kholodov. I cannot forgive someone who offended Angelica, be it her son or god himself."

"It's very convenient," Eugene says, breaking into a playful smile, "because you don't know the former at all and don't believe in the latter."

"I believe," Adeline says, "that it's a beautiful evening, and you won't be able to overshadow our joy with your caustic remarks. Do you agree, Angelica?"

Madam Lissova nods and raises her contemplative gaze to the sky.

"Mariinsky is unlike any other theatre," she says. "See how the rays of the sunset shimmer on its malachite vaults—how beautiful is its light-emerald façade and rounded dome! Even the most ardent fire could not consume it entirely. I often imagine this divine building engulfed in flames. Beauty must die beautifully. This is what we are going to witness today. Right, Margarita?"

"Angelica, you are incredible!" Adeline says. "Is it possible to talk so ominously about a performance that we are going to see for the first time?" The way she looks at Madam Lissova lights a fire deep in my chest.

"Believe me, Adeline, we live in such a performance every day without noticing it." Madam Lissova turns around and rushes to the front entrance of the theatre. We follow the long train of her dress and find ourselves in a spacious hall.

Just like she said, Mariinsky bewilders its first-time visitors. There is no red velvet garnish and no heavy curtains. Instead of the usual dark, imposing colours, we see pale mint walls and turquoise vaults decorated with the smooth white sculptures of seraphim.

We enter a gigantic cloakroom and get lost in the couture of socialites who want to get rid of their expensive fur coats for the duration of the ballet.

Madam Lissova greets acquaintances and smiles. Meanwhile, Misha is building another revolutionary plan, preparing to disrupt his mother's escape.

How painful it must be to hide behind a mask all your life! I think, watching her eyes glaze over with haughty indifference.

Adeline's cloak, like a wild burgundy orchid, falls from her shoulders. Her blue satin gown captures everyone's attention.

"You dressed to match the Mariinsky Theatre," says Madam Lissova.

"You are teasing me!" Adeline chuckles.

"Soon, you will see what I mean."

Following Madam Lisova, we head to our seats. Angelica is the first to present her ticket and enter the box, the most expensive one, opposite the "tsar" box, where the Emperor and his family settle to watch the ballet.

"This is incredible!" Adeline presses her hands to her chest and turns around as if inviting me to share her delight. "I love these colours—navy blue, azure, and gold trim everywhere!"

"I'm glad you like it," I say, trying not to show my embarrassment.

I have always wanted to become a part of this world, but it is foreign to me. This sparkling dream, in which Adeline and Madam Lissova feel at home, evades my spirit. I can never let it guide me because I love the call of the North Wind, the cracked ice on the Neva, and the song of the nightingale on a humid, white night.

Kholodov, grinning at the opportunity to "spend time with three charming ladies," as he announced upon his arrival, proudly takes the seat next to Madam Lissova.

I stay beside Adeline. The dim theatre lighting accentuates the curves of my lace-collared, sea-green dress—finally, I have an occasion to wear it.

"Margo, you look dazzling!" Adeline exclaims.

"And so do you."

Adeline's dark-blue satin gown with golden embroidery encircling her waist and chest reminds me of the starry night that envelops Saint Petersburg in its misty embrace.

My eyes absorb the grotesque luxury of the regal theatre space, from its wide stage crowned by the gold-framed clock to the dramatic splendour of the angel murals above it. Our box allows for a spectacular view of the centre stage, and I watch the candles flicker while the orchestra rehearses the "Danse des petits cygnes."

"I have been meaning to apologize—I hope I did not get you into too much trouble last night by taking you home," Adeline whispers.

"Oh, not at all!" I reply, looking at the magnificent theatre ceiling, where cherubs dance around the crystal chandelier, holding hands in the azure-blue sky.

"Mariinsky is a masterpiece in and of itself," she notes, "to think that we are going to see and hear yet another masterpiece in this magical place is pure paradise. I'm so happy you joined me, Margo!"

"Anna Pavlova is going to perform 'The Dying Swan' dance for the first time tonight," Madam Lissova adds, "this talented young woman will transform the art of ballet, mark my words!"

"All great art is inspired by poetry," Adeline says. "Do you remember the wild swan's death-hymn?" She turns to Madam Lissova.

"Of course, I remember this poem—it's Tennyson." Madam Lissova nods.

"Which is worse—joy in the wasteland or sorrow in paradise?" Adeline asks, tilting her head.

"Joy passes quickly. Sorrow is eternal. You and I know this all too well," Madam Lissova replies.

"What a gruesome conversation!" Kholodov interrupts, "I, for one, cannot help but rejoice because remarkable women surround me tonight," he adds, attempting to imitate Adeline's British accent.

She sneers, but Eugene goes on with childlike delight.

"Marvellous! Marvellous!" he shouts. "If only I had known years ago that one toast would land me in such splendid company, I would have toasted to you every day, Madam Lissova."

"Be careful with your praise, my dear Dr. Kholodov, for even the most subtle flattery must have its limits," Adeline warns.

Eugene glances at her but lowers his gaze to the brochure in his lap as soon as her onyx eyes pierce him.

"What a woman!" Kholodov whispers to Madam Lissova, "No, but have you heard—*the most subtle flattery?* What a woman she is, your Miss Daze!"

Eugene cannot finish his thought because the curtain rises, and a round of deafening applause fills the Mariinsky. When the theatre grows silent, the exquisite sound of the flute emerges from the orchestra pit. The violins and the oboe expand this delicate melody in a transcendent symphony of a midnight forest.

I follow the rhythm of the entrancing music, hypnotized by the dazzling magic of the Mariinsky Theatre. I feel Mariinsky's heartbeat with every cell of my body—its melody multiplies sorrow and happiness, transforming them into an invisible painting with colours that can only be felt, not seen. The prima ballerina begins her hypnotizing dance in the mist surrounding the royal domain.

By the frozen lake, Odette meets the evil sorcerer who turns her into a swan, and the tale begins. Dozens of lightweight girls soar above the stage in their feathery snow-white tutus, and I watch their graceful movements in silent awe. It takes great strength to move this effortlessly, like the spirits of the North Wind themselves, becoming one with the music.

Adeline tilts her head, admiring the dancers. As the ballet goes on, I find it harder and harder to resist looking at her. Her reactions to the performance are almost more enticing than the ballet itself.

The Black Swan enters the stage in a vertiginous pirouette, and I tremble, looking at her sapphire crown.

Odile—Odette's malicious twin—seduces the Prince, and the Swan Queen weeps: the pain of betrayal reflects in the wild abruptness of her movements.

If even the most beautiful swan mourns betrayal, why do we believe in love at all? White and Black, Yin and Yang, the light of hope and the all-encompassing darkness of loss seduce us into their flaming chaos. Angelica is right: we are all spinning in this dance—the dance of life and death—from which no one can emerge victorious.

The curtain falls—Act I is over.

I turn to glance at Kholodov—when everyone stands up, one of the ushers approaches him with a handwritten note. Eugene turns pale and disappears without a word.

"Your companion has left you, Angelica," Adeline says, grinning at her, "he must have found his Odile!"

"There is one advantage to being old—you stop taking things personally," Lissova says. "And when someone leaves—you let them." She smiles and walks out into the gallery.

"Kholodov received a note. What could it be?" I ask Adeline.

"It was something gruesome, no doubt," she says. "How do you say it? The less you know—the better you sleep."

"Curiosity doesn't let me sleep," I say, "and don't we always find out the truth in the end?"

"I suggest we check out the buffet." Adeline stands up. "Kholodov's mysteries do not interest me. He is trying to wear the mask of a tormented genius who thinks he can get drunk at Angelica's charitable parties without consequences. Madam Lissova always remains too kind to people who do not deserve her."

I follow Adeline to the theatre bar. After studying the wine list, she orders two glasses of Pinot Noir.

"To 'Swan Lake'!" she says. We clink glasses, and I close my eyes, taking a sip of the dark-ruby liquid.

"Champagne in the afternoon, wine in the evening—we are living like the Romanovs—but only for tonight," Adeline muses. "Have you seen the Emperor's face?" she asks me.

I think for a moment, envisioning the deep shadow of the "tsar" box, but the faces escape me—the Emperor's presence is a mere apparition floating above the audience. There is nothing real and grounded about men who start senseless wars—they are shadows with forgettable auras. Their souls are never profound enough to make a lasting impression.

"I haven't seen him—not tonight," I say, shaking my head.

"Some other night then?" Adeline laughs. "What a strange woman you are!"

"Not stranger than you!" I say, gazing at her ruby earrings, resplendent in the bar's dim light.

"Rumour has it, Tsar Nicholas is away at his Summer Residence in Tsarskoye Selo," Adeline says, lowering her voice. "The protests have scared him," she whispers, and I have to lean in before the noise of the theatre crowd carries her words away.

"He has no reason to fear," I say. "The executioners are doing their job just fine." My hand shakes, and I put my wine glass down.

"Listen to me," Adeline says, covering my hand with hers. "You don't need the crowds to take him down. You only need one man as powerful and stubborn as him. This is what always happens. The crowd is nothing—character is everything."

"And so we will have another ruler who destroys the country, feasting on the bones of his predecessor." I sigh.

"Or you will finally taste freedom!" she says, smiling at me. "I felt it at Angelica's ball when I was waltzing with you. You set me free after years of mental isolation—I could not touch a living thing without pain, and you made me forget it."

"Or," I tease her, "you simply enjoy dancing."

"You are a cunning fox!" she bursts out laughing. "Of course, I enjoy it—dancing with you."

"Adeline," I say with a shadow of hesitation, "I haven't told you the whole truth about what happened last night."

"So tell me," she says, watching the red streaks forming on the edges of her glass—"are you in trouble, after all?"

"The woman you saw yesterday… she was my lover," I confess, "but now she's gone—perhaps, forever—to a lover of her own."

"Love… this is exactly why I don't believe in it!" Adeline frowns. "You think you know someone, and then, one day—"

"No," I say, "this has been going on for a long time, and my late return has just sped up what was bound to happen anyway."

"Are you glad she is gone, then?" Adeline rests her chin on her hand, looking at me with curiosity.

"I am finally free," I say, lowering my head.

"Then use your freedom." She strokes my hair away from my eyes. Bewildered, I gaze at her parted lips.

The theatre bell rings two times.

Adeline tips the bartender, and we head back to our seats.

I lightly brush my fingers against the luscious satin of her dress before sitting down. Madam Lissova notices my poorly concealed gesture. Her silver-blonde head turns in our direction. Golden flecks of curiosity melt in the tempestuous depths of her half-closed eyes.

Adeline glances at me, lightly touching my wrist.

"Did you enjoy the intermission?" Madam Lissova's voice interrupts our silent exchange.

"You should have joined us!" Adeline replies, turning around to smile at her. "The bar has excellent wine, which is a rarity in a theatre."

"My own company suits me quite well," Madam Lissova says, shaking her head. "I am comfortable being alone because solitude has always been my faithful companion." She grins, looking at Kholodov's empty seat. "He left us so quickly! Have you heard him whispering about death, Margarita?"

"I haven't heard a thing," I say, remembering Kholodov's words about Adeline. Something terrible must have happened to take him away from the three women he enjoyed watching more than "Swan Lake."

"I am sure this ballet has bored him to death!" Adeline grins, and her teeth gleam like a flash of lightning in the midst of a theatre plunging into darkness.

"What else could I expect from a physics professor?" Madam Lissova sighs. "But he was very agitated."

"On the bright side, you do not have to worry about him now," Adeline says in her deep, enveloping voice. "In fact, don't worry about anything at all, my dear."

They exchange warm, reassuring glances, and I feel another burn of inexplicable jealousy.

Madam Lissova and Adeline will go to Paris together—without me, I think, and tears fill my eyes.

Act II begins.

Adeline gasps when the Prince embraces the Black Swan, and the two merge in a dizzying dance. The powerful soundwaves reflect from floor to ceiling as the ballet reaches its climax—the sorcerer finds Odette and takes her life.

When Pavlova emerges on stage as the dying swan, the music sways her in its desolate rhythm, encompassing her body the way an oceanic wind carries the strong-winged albatross into the eye of the storm.

The melody reminds me of the day I met Sophia—when the North Wind lifted and carried away her black veil, and her amber eyes filled with tenderness as she clasped her hands around my waist.

I see her standing in the beam of light with only a white silk nightgown protecting her from the blizzard. The storm winnows Sophia's raven locks. She trembles on the edge of the windowsill, preparing to jump. Desolate cries escape her chest. Sophia's eyes wander: the eternal winter stretches out before her in its midnight-black gown—one moment separates her from its dark embrace. Only one moment.

Take care of your loved ones, Margarita! whispers the North Wind.

Sophia jumps out of the window, and the silk of her nightgown flutters like an angelic train behind her. Akin to a bird that has forgotten its wings, my love shatters on the ground.

"Sophia," I shout through the music, "Sophia!" A gust of wind carries me to the stage, and I freeze over her body, buried in the blood-red snow. I touch her shoulders, cold and still, like in that nightmare where I wake up in our icy bed and see her lifeless eyes turned to me in silent prayer.

I try to lift Sophia and call for help, but the ice cracks under my feet, and a terrible abyss pulls her from my hands. I fall through the ice with her, and the arctic waves close over us, clouding my eyes with a crimson veil. I push through the water and grab Sophia's arm again. Her body, emaciated and unearthly light, follows me with ghostly obedience. I see a distant light breaking through the thick wall of freezing water, but my lungs run out of air, and my mind melts into a cloud of icy mist.

"Why have you done this, Sophia? Why have you done this?" I repeat, unable to fight the current.

"Margo… Margo!" Adeline's warm whisper makes me come to my senses. I realize that I have been squeezing her hand tightly all this time. I release her wrist from my death grip and exhale slowly.

"I'm sorry!" I blush and try to focus on the scene where Anna Pavlova is still performing the dance of the dying swan. My hallucinatory attack must have lasted no more than a minute, but it seems that an eternity has passed. I still see Sophia's black curls drowning in the crimson snow.

Adeline runs her fingers through my hair without saying a word as if she wanted to make me forget the pain spreading through my body and mind like poison.

I'll take care of you, her gentle gesture says. Struck by a wave of tenderness, I freeze from this unexpected touch. I turn around and notice tears rolling down her pale cheeks.

Pavlova spins in a final pirouette—the white, silky wings damaged by cruel witchcraft cannot lift her. Odette's tender heart, once racing, skips a beat. Her feathers, airy and soft, wrap around her body when she collapses to the ground.

The orchestra thunders in agony—the swan takes its last breath.

"Bravo!" the audience chants. "Bravo!"

Roars of applause and enthusiastic shouts fill the Mariinsky Theatre.

Adeline holds out her hand to me.

"Are you okay, Margo? Forgive me for asking you this. I

still cannot forgive myself for what happened at the ball."

"I just need some fresh air," I reassure her, my head still spinning from the vivid nightmare.

Sophia is dead, whispers the North Wind. *Sophia is dead.*

Adeline stands up without letting go of my hand. "Angelica, will you look after her while I retrieve our clothes from the cloakroom?" she says.

Madam Lissova nods and helps me up.

"The performance was long and very intense, my dear—no wonder you are exhausted," she tells me when we walk out into the gallery, and Adeline disappears among the colourful coats and hats.

"On the contrary, I feel full of life!" I say, holding on to the railing to keep my balance. A strange tremor penetrating my body to the very bones makes me stagger.

She is dead because of you, howls the hoarse voice of the North Wind. *Dead. Because of you.*

"Do you hear it?" I try to suppress a sob bursting out of my chest.

"Hear what, my darling?" Madam Lissova asks, listening to the rumble of a snowstorm outside the high theatre windows. "The weather is getting nastier each day," she says.

"No, that voice—"

"You must have heard the screams of the protesters!" She

smiles. "Don't be afraid. They won't be able to approach the Mariinsky. Our mighty Emperor has posted his loyal guards all around the building—after all, his family is here."

"Family," I repeat. "Mom always dreamt of visiting the Mariinsky Theatre."

"Dreamt? Why are you talking as if she were—"

"Ah! I don't know—I don't know." Tears fill my eyes, and Madam Lissova hugs me.

"Everyone leaves and everyone dies—everyone!" I whisper.

"Calm down, Margarita! I know—it's all Adeline's fault. She is trying to intoxicate you, put you under her spell—but don't give in." Madam Lissova laughs. A shadow falls over her thin face. "You cannot imagine how cruel she can be."

"Why do you think she is cruel?" I blurt out. "After all, she loved you! I'm sure she still loves you. It was you who were cruel to her—you left her!"

"Silly, silly girl," she whispers with a bitter smile, "you'll understand everything soon enough."

Offended by her words, I break free from Lissova's arms.

"What do I have to understand?"

"I suspect Adeline hasn't told you everything about our summer in Paris," Madam Lissova says. "You are as ardent as my son, Margarita. I know you won't listen to me, but did Adeline tell you that the very summer our romance began, she was to marry a nobleman?"

"Your romance? So you *did* love her back?" My heart sinks. All this time, I imagined the cold, unapproachable Madam Lissova and the meek, submissive Adeline, burdened with the curse of unrequited love, which the Russian aristocrat fed by leading her on in every possible way.

"Ha! She didn't tell you that, either?" Angelica looks at me with a knowing smile. I shake my head.

"So Adeline got married? This is impossible to believe! I can't imagine her with a man. When did you find out she was engaged?" I try to take a breath, but the bitterness of confusion and resentment smothers me.

"I did not find out right away," Madam Lissova says. "You see—I had a plan. I wanted to leave Dmitry and escape from this strange luxurious life where I could never find happiness. My husband knew about everything from the very beginning of the marriage. In other words, he understood that I could never fulfill all the usual duties of a wife. Our marriage became a flexible arrangement, but ever since I met Adeline, I stopped lying to myself. I have always wanted to be free, and I wanted to share this freedom with her. We could have lived in Paris!" Sparks of joy flare in Madam Lissova's eyes.

"You have no idea how much I dreamt about it!" she exclaims. "I'm ashamed to admit it, but I was ready to leave

Misha for her. I have never been a good mother. But Adeline... she told me about her engagement on the night of our elopement." Lissova turns away from me. "I still can't forgive her—and myself, too. She was an eighteen-year-old girl—of course, she was scared to change her life like that for a woman she barely knew."

I listen to Madam Lissova with bated breath.

"What happened? Did she call off the engagement?"

"Adeline did something much better—she left her fiancé right at the altar. She wrote about it in a letter, but it was too late—Dmitry and I had already returned to Russia, and I could not trust her again."

"She hasn't told me anything about all of this!" I look into Madam Lissova's eyes, trying to find a hint of deceit, but her gaze remains clear, glowing with tears.

"You are very young," Madam Lissova says, "and youth is a strange time. Everyone will tell you it's the best part of your life. Don't believe it for a second. There is no better or worse time. We all live as well as we can, regardless of age."

"I am sure Adeline feels sorry for betraying you," I say, "and that's why she didn't tell me anything. It is very embarrassing and painful for her to remember the engagement and your failed elopement—do you understand?"

"I warned you," Madam Lissova says, shaking my hand

with a sigh of regret, "but that's it. I have to find my son."

"If we don't see each other again, please, tell him that he will always remain my friend, no matter what," I beg her.

Madam Lissova nods. Sorrow flickers in her eyes, but the usual icy serenity replaces it when Adeline returns from the wardrobe with our coats.

I want to shower Adeline with questions, but Madam Lissova unfolds the evening paper left by one of the theatre spectators.

"How horrible!" she screams and throws the newspaper on the table.

Adeline and I freeze, amazed at such a violent reaction.

"What's wrong?" Adeline asks.

"Somebody has murdered Dr. Novikov." Madam Lissova comes to her senses and shows us the headline.

"Novikov? Murdered?" I ask. Fear envelops my words.

Of course, Novikov's fate does not matter to me, but what about Sophia—my poor Sophia? After all, she went to him last night! What will become of her?

"Don't listen to Angelica," Adeline says, shaking her head. "We have seen enough deaths today!"

"It happened last night," Lissova reads. "In the early morning, eyewitnesses noticed a woman—"

"Aren't you ashamed of reading this in front of Margo?"

Adeline interrupts. "Can't you see that she isn't feeling well? Why does the poor girl need to know about another death after such a tragic ballet?"

"Oh, forget the ballet, Adeline! Do you remember how Kholodov spoke about Novikov at my ball?" Lissova arches her eyebrow. "Don't you think him receiving this strange note is another suspicious coincidence? On the night of the ball, he left before everyone else and was horribly drunk, remember?"

"Well, he left after Misha, who, by the way, you still need to find," Adeline reminds her. "I guarantee you, Angelica—the police will take care of everything."

"Of course," Madam Lissova says, curbing her ardour, "of course. We'll see each other again soon, won't we, Adeline?"

"Yes—at the station, the day after tomorrow."

"Ah… the day after tomorrow!" After thinking for a second, Madam Lissova holds out her hand to me. "Farewell, Margarita. Take care of yourself."

"Good night to you," I reply.

Lissova's light silhouette dissolves among hundreds of dressed-up ladies and gentlemen leaving the theatre.

"Margo," Adeline begins, but I interrupt her.

"You have been lying to me all this time, haven't you?"

"Lying to you?" Adeline freezes in bewilderment. "What are you talking about?"

"I am talking about your cancelled wedding," I yell. "Madam Lissova has told me everything—you betrayed her, *you!*"

"Please, calm down," she says. "Would you like a glass of water?"

At the snap of her fingers, one of the doormen runs up to us and, blushing deeply and apologetically, asks, "What can I do for you?"

"Bring us some water, please," I grumble. My throat feels dry from the terrible news.

"You are angry with me—I understand," Adeline chirps, accepting a glass of ice-cold water from the porter's hands, "but come to your senses! All evening long Angelica did nothing but try to drive wedges between us. Didn't you notice her ambiguous looks and smiles? I knew not to leave the two of you alone."

"She was completely sincere!" I snatch the glass from Adeline's hands and take a greedy sip to extinguish the fire of anger that has flared up inside me.

"Yes," Adeline says, "she sincerely wants to get rid of you—her rival—after all, you have endeared her closest people to you—Mikhail and myself. We both know she has no one else left."

"You are a very cruel woman, after all!" I say. My cheeks

burn with resentment, and I throw the remaining cold water in her face.

Adeline closes her eyes. She remains motionless for a few moments. The realization of what I have done comes over me.

"I am so sorry!" I take a step back. "I have been hurting you all day," I say. My words seem like a distant echo, as if it's not me speaking at all, but my shadow.

I expect Adeline to pounce on me, but she calmly takes a handkerchief and wipes her cheekbones, glistening with water.

"It's alright," she says, "you are very tired. I should have gotten you out of here back when you grabbed my arm during the second act and started calling someone by name."

"Sophia," I say, swallowing nervously, "I called Sophia, the same woman who left me... for Novikov."

"So that's what it was!" Adeline gasps. "Is that the reason why you were so moved by his death?"

"Yes. You see, I need to get back as soon as possible—I am sure Sophia is alone in our apartment now and doesn't know what to do. She doesn't have anyone else! I must help her, because—"

"Margo," Adeline says, putting her hands on my shoulders. "Stop. You're not going anywhere—and certainly not to your apartment. You are saying she most likely returned there after spending the night with Novikov, right?"

"Yes," I pause. "We had an argument last night, and she said she was going to his apartment."

"You are a smart young woman," Adeline says, "You must understand that the authorities will search your apartment soon. Given your connection to Sophia, your return may put her and yourself in even greater danger. Have you heard what's going on in the streets? People are screaming that the Emperor has left the Empire—the government may collapse at any moment. I won't let you go. Not on this fateful night."

I swallow my tears. Adeline is right, but I don't want to admit it.

"What should we do then?" I ask.

"You can spend the night with me," Adeline says, squeezing my hands. "Oh dear, you are cold as ice!"

I lower my gaze. Despite Madam Lissova's words, I want to believe that Adeline has changed. I treated her terribly, and she still invited me to her place. A truly cruel, deceitful woman wouldn't do that.

"Here," Adeline says, taking off her burgundy cloak and draping it over my shoulders. "It will keep you warm."

"I had a vision," I whisper, "that Sophia committed suicide."

"It was only a vision, my dear. You care about her because she was part of your heart." Adeline pats my back. "You need to let her go—forever."

Wrapped in the soft warmth of Adeline's cloak, I no longer resist her words.

"I will try."

Whatever you say, Adeline—I will do whatever you say.

Together, we leave the Mariinsky Theatre, embraced by the deep northern night.

"Just look at this!" Adeline points to the North Star twinkling above our heads, surrounded by its less luminous sisters.

"Even the stars need company," I say, admiring the gentle glow of their heavenly eyes.

"When I look at the stars," Adeline says, "I imagine that each of them is a moment of happiness in the infinite ocean of grief. No matter what happens, remember that moments like these make life worth living."

Chapter 7:
My Creature Fair

Her beauty flares as if about to drown...
January 11, Midnight

Adeline and I skirr past the busy streets. The waves of civil unrest and fires cover Saint Petersburg. Usually quiet and unhurried, the cold northern night turns into a cavalcade of flashes and shouts, among which I hear a unanimous call: "Down with the Emperor!"

Wrapped in Adeline's burgundy cloak, I snuggle up to her in the carriage that takes us to the outskirts of the city—to the wasteland where the train station is located.

"The inn I'm staying at," Adeline says, "is next to the railroad so that the guests can immediately get on their train. It took me a long time to get used to the constant rumble and whistles, but now I love this melody of movement and change."

"Ah, you are a real revolutionary!" I laugh, and she presses her finger to her lips.

The inn turns out to be small and not at all as luxurious as I imagined. My eyes do not detect any chandeliers, heavy curtains, or shuffling doormen.

"Margo will be my guest for the night. Could you bring something warm to our room?" Adeline asks a tall receptionist in a worn-out three-piece suit.

"Vodka? Wine?" The receptionist raises his eyebrows and looks at me in disbelief.

"What would you like?" Adeline asks me.

Still shivering from the cold, I remember what she ordered at the theatre.

"Pinot Noir," I answer with hesitation.

"Bring us a bottle of Pinot Noir," Adeline commands and takes my arm as she rushes down the long corridor of hotel suites.

Finally, she opens the door of the "Empress Suite," and I enter a spacious living room.

"There are so many candles here!" I say, covering my eyes. "I feel like I have stepped into a cathedral."

The smooth glow of the flames makes my head spin.

"My maid lights them every night before I return," Adeline

says, taking off my cloak. "Make yourself at home. There is a fireplace in the bedroom if you want to warm up."

"It's very kind of you," I say, blushing, "but I feel good here, too."

"No one stays at this inn for long," Adeline says, "but as you can see, I still managed to furnish the interior to my liking." She shows me around the suite.

Her writing desk, fenced off by a dark violet screen, stands in front of the high window, behind which I can hear the trains passing by, their metallic bodies roaring as they cut through the thick layers of ice and snow. On the other side of the screen is the dark living room sheltered from daylight. Freshly lit candles flicker on mahogany chests of drawers. Their flames reflect in antique mirrors hung on each wall next to gold-framed portraits of women in Victorian dresses.

A miniature coffee table and two gloomy velvet armchairs sit on a Persian rug in the midst of this mysterious chiaroscuro space.

"I spent so much time persuading the innkeeper to hang them!" Adeline sighs, pointing at the paintings.

"They are gorgeous," I say, holding a candelabra to one of the canvases—a portrait of a tall blonde woman in a purple dress. She looks a lot like Angelica.

"My mother is a famous London artist," Adeline says.

She is standing behind me, and I feel the delicate satin of her evening gown brush lightly against my thigh.

"So all these paintings are her work?"

"Yes. She draws the British nobility, but sometimes comes down to earth with more intimate paintings of her loved ones," Adeline says. "I can show you a portrait she did of me ages ago."

Adeline leads me to the corner where a small canvas depicts a thin girl in a flowing white dress. She is walking down the garden path abloom with wild orchids and irises. It is impossible to recognize the woman standing beside me in the girl's angular silhouette.

"What do you think?" Adeline asks. Her half-demonic smile grows colder at my silence.

I study the picture. The girl's pale skin and dark beaconing eyes, round like ripe cherries, make my skin crawl.

"She doesn't look like you at all," I say finally.

"Are you sure?" Adeline brings the candle to the painting, and, for a second, it seems that the portrait will flare up. "Do you think I've changed?" she whispers.

"My mother is an artist, too," I say instead of answering her question. "However, she likes to paint landscapes more than people."

"It's a pity!" Adeline shakes her head. "Only the human

personality can inspire a true masterpiece! Don't you think that all writers, artists, and poets use people as copies from which they draw their creations?" Adeline's voice trembles in time with the candle's flame.

"This is a very cynical view of creativity," I say, trying to look for the familiar warmth in her gaze, but it dissipates in the strange cold trance when Adeline admires the paintings. "Do you think your mother used you as a copy, too?"

"Yes—she used me as an imperfect copy of herself!" Adeline laughs, and the icy cracks of pain splinter her laughter in half. "You may call me cold and cynical, but I am only saying what I had learned a long time ago. People use each other for mutual benefit, and it is excellent when something beautiful comes out of it, like these paintings."

I want to argue with her, but my eyes stop at the bookshelves by her bedroom door.

"I forgot to return your poetry collection!" I say.

"There is no need to return the book to me," Adeline says, smiling. "I'm sure it has found a more worthy home in your hands. Do you remember what Keats wrote about the 'fair creature of an hour'?"

"Ah, yes—this is one of my favourite sonnets!"

A knock on the door interrupts me, and a scowling girl in a snow-white cap enters the room with a delayed, apologetic smile. She puts a bottle of wine and two glasses on the round table in the living room and disappears without accepting Adeline's generous tip.

"I must say, the local servants never cease to amaze me!" Adeline exclaims. "How is it possible to refuse well-deserved money with such pride?"

"Isn't it obvious?" I say. "This girl despises us, and I understand her perfectly."

"What is there to understand?" Adeline says, grinning at me. "She does her job well, and I want to reward her. You just like arguing, Margo."

"You will never understand it," I say. "It's hard for you to realize that others didn't have the same opportunities as you—you could never feel the way they feel, especially at times like these."

"My family has never been poor," Adeline says, frowning, "but this does not mean that I am devoid of empathy or human understanding. If I were born a peasant, I would accept help from everyone, making any concessions in order to improve my situation. Pride is a privilege. Do you understand? It has to be earned."

I shake my head as I pour Pinot Noir into our glasses.

"Do you want to attack me again?" Adeline laughs. "You accused me of lying, so I am telling you the truth as it is."

"It's not the truth—it's just your opinion," I say.

With a smile, Adeline nods and takes the glass from my outstretched hand. Sparks of curiosity and wild amusement ignite in her eyes.

"Who would have thought that the inhabitants of a country that keeps everyone's mouth shut could be so sharp-tongued?" Adeline says, raising her glass. "As a sharp-tongued woman myself, I quite like it."

"You are a terrible woman, Adeline," I say through gritted teeth.

Madam Lissova's words echo in my mind.

You can't imagine how cruel she can be.

"Well, let's drink to terrible women—and to you, my fair creature," Adeline says, sipping her wine.

Why do I have to accept this? I think. *First, she gives me gifts, then feeds me lies, and now invites me to spend the night with her, calling me a "fair creature."*

I don't know if I hate Adeline or admire her.

"Help yourself," she says, opening a box of marzipan fruit from Eliseeff's Emporium. I freeze, unable to look at her.

As if reading my mind, Adeline sighs. "I know I have to tell you everything." Her gaze wanders over me as if trying to cling to the lace of my dress. "Trust me: I haven't told you about the broken wedding because I didn't want to complicate things between us. In other words, I didn't think you would want to know... about my past."

"But I want to know!" I say, gazing at her with unfathomable hunger in my eyes. "I want to know everything about you."

"You are too impatient," Adeline says. "We have the whole night ahead of us." She puts her glass on the table. "Where should I begin?"

"Start with your engagement. Why didn't you tell Angelica that you had a fiancé?" I ask.

"It won't be easy," Adeline says, meeting my gaze with a regretful smile, "but I will try to tell you everything. After all, you deserve to hear the truth."

I bite into a marzipan peach and feel the powdered sugar dribbling from its ruddy flesh. With each sip of wine, I become more and more immersed in the atmosphere of a strange French fairy tale inspired by Adeline. Her velvety, insinuating voice fills the room.

"So, Angelica has told you everything about my betrayal," Adeline says. "Has she mentioned that I informed her about the upcoming wedding an hour before our supposed escape?"

I nod. Electrifying silence fills the room before Adeline leans back and begins her story. Her eyelids tremble with tension, and I see with what painful meticulousness she picks every word.

"That spring, in Paris, a gentleman proposed to me. He was a wealthy aristocrat and a close friend of my parents—a perfect match! I felt deep affection for him, but nothing more. I have been in love many times, but I could never love a human being the way I loved poetry, the lullaby of the wind, or the Siberian kitten I sheltered from the winter storm."

"Are you telling me you never loved Angelica?" I ask.

"I did not know her long enough to love her." Adeline shakes her head. "My feelings have always been like clouds: they form and dissipate on their own—too fast, perhaps, to create anything meaningful."

"I find all of this hard to believe," I say, crossing my arms.

"Are you calling me a liar again?" Adeline laughs, but I can see pain and anger lurking in the darkness of her gaze.

"Even if you are telling me the truth, you are lying to yourself."

She pauses. Her eyes pierce me like the sharpest steel.

"You are very perceptive," Adeline says, emptying her glass, "and nothing seems to scare you."

"Nothing." I look at her lips, red with wine, and hear the trains passing high above as if we were submerged beneath the sea, listening to the endless hum of the earthly world through the thick wall of salt water.

"Well," she continues, "My fiancé's name was Raphael

Gravier. All the women in Paris were crazy about him—a young poet with eyes brighter than wild cornflowers and jet black hair that reached his shoulders. The son of eminent diplomats, Raphael devoted his life to art. Young and naïve, I fell in love with him. But, as I told you before, such feelings never lingered in my heart for long. Raphael and I grew up together, and he was a true friend to me long before our mutual romantic attraction. On my eighteenth birthday, the young poet admitted that he always saw me as his future wife. It was not a shock to anyone who knew us, and, not yet knowing what life had in store for me, I gladly accepted his offer. I saw how other women looked at Raphael, and I wanted him to belong to me alone."

"But love is not about power and possession," I interrupt her. "Didn't you understand this?"

"What else can a young woman from a wealthy family understand about love?" Adeline says. "The upper-class life isolated me from the world, so possession and power were all I knew about feelings. My parents weren't affectionate with each other, and I had never seen my father kiss my mother or show any sympathy for her. He was a real tyrant, and I am glad that I managed to get out of my parents' nest by entering the Sorbonne."

"If their marriage was so horrible," I say, "why have you

chosen the same path for yourself?"

"I wanted to build my own life," Adeline says. "Having seen enough of the suffering my parents went through, I decided that my marriage would be different, that I could choose a betrothed among my friends—someone who would not control and humiliate me—someone who would provide me with freedom. Raphael was like that, but we were only children when we dreamt of marrying each other."

"Did he know about Angelica?" I ask, covering my mouth with my hand as I imagine Adeline accepting the marriage proposal.

"No," she says slowly. "He did not know and will never know."

Adeline sips from her glass and closes her eyes. I can see that these memories cause her incredible pain.

"Please continue," I plead, kneeling by her armchair. Her voice attracts me like a siren's lure.

"The engagement took place in March," she says, reaching out to stroke my hair. "Our families had scheduled the wedding for late September. Everyone was overjoyed. Just think—I could have become the omnipotent Adeline Gravier, mingling with the French high society and giving lavish receptions while my husband wrote poetry in his study overlooking the Seine. And then I met Angelica. I could never imagine that my feelings for a woman could be stronger than what I felt for Raphael. To tell you the truth, I had doubts even before meeting her and rarely wore the wedding ring. After Angelica and I met at the fair, my double life began. All the feelings I had for my blue-eyed prince melted like spring ice when I realized I could be much happier with this charming, wise, intelligent woman."

My eyes widen in astonishment. "And your fiancé didn't suspect a thing?" I ask.

"This young man has never cared about anything or anyone too deeply," Adeline says, "but, of course, he became jealous of my non-existent admirers. Raphael even threatened to terminate the engagement. He used to spend hours looking for me at night, searching through every bar and restaurant in Paris while I lingered in the spacious house of the Russian aristocrat, surrounded by thousands of books Dmitry brought from Saint Petersburg. Angelica used to read to me in Russian, and I listened, enchanted by her voice. Dmitry visited his wife very rarely, always busy conducting all sorts of political negotiations, which Angelica and I did not care about."

"And it didn't scare you that she was older than you?" I ask. "Weren't you afraid she was only playing with your feelings?" I sit down on the floor near Adeline's feet and marvel at the scarlet patterns on the Persian rug. My heart races as I await her reply.

"No, I wasn't afraid," Adeline says. Her eyes are dark with thought. "Strangely," she whispers, "I felt at peace."

She pauses, running her fingers through my hair. "Due to the evenings with Angelica, I realized what my heart desired—mutual understanding and acceptance, which have not been present in my relationship with Raphael. Everything was a game with him. Angelica, on the contrary, encompassed all the qualities that I so desperately aspired to possess. I never got tired of her company. I didn't have to figure out what to do or how to behave, as I did when men pursued me. Life seemed easy and free with her. We would go to the Louvre, buy fresh croissants, and spend the night out on her spacious balcony, counting the stars. It felt so right—so universally perfect!" Adeline shakes her head, trying to hide the tears glimmering in her eyes.

"If you really felt this way about Angelica, why didn't you tell her about Raphael?" My hand clenches into a fist. "You are evading the truth again."

"You are right. My actions are difficult to justify," Adeline says, lowering her gaze, "but can you imagine what state I was in? I confessed my feelings to Angelica without mentioning Raphael because I was not ready to exchange the stable future of a socialite for that all-consuming sense of inner freedom.

What I felt for her was difficult and inexplicable for such a young heart. These intense desires frightened me then and continue to oppress my soul even now. My rational mind recognized that it was wrong and reckless to leave everything for Angelica, who burst into my life like a thunderstorm amid the darkest winter."

"Why?" I keep asking. "If you really cared for Angelica, you could have confessed to everything and told her you were not ready. Why didn't you spare her heart? I want to understand you, Adeline."

"I loved both Angelica and Raphael in my own way," she says. "I did not want to lose them—but how would that be possible? When I was eighteen, I did not know two women could be together and love freely. My feelings for Angelica would have led me to the dark, frightening abyss. I wanted our fleeting happiness to last as long as possible, so I made Angelica believe that I was ready to run away with her. Otherwise, she would have stopped our meetings, saying that we have no future. Do you understand?" Adeline pours wine into my glass.

"Yes, but that doesn't make your actions any less cruel." I take a deep breath, trying to calm my heart.

"You can judge me," Adeline says, "but I couldn't find any other way. These were the happiest days of my life, about which poets so often write. I knew that running away would mean expulsion from Parisian society for both of us. Why would I ruin our lives like that? It's irresponsible. You Russians are endowed with the spirit of romanticism, and I envy it, but the heart cannot win where the mind rules."

"So you were afraid of public opinion?" I ask. "There is nothing logical and reasonable in what you describe. This is plain cowardice," I say, standing up to face her. Adeline bares her teeth, staring at me with indignation.

"How could you think of such a hurtful explanation? You can't accuse me of cowardice without knowing a fraction of what I've been through," she snaps. "I felt that it was wrong to love someone who condemned me to an eternal existence in the shadows—in the endless secrecy from which we would not be able to escape."

"Just admit you regret it," I say, shaking my head. Adeline lets out a frustrated sigh.

"One day, you will realize that this was the only way out," she says. "Angelica, with her distressed marriage and the little child in her arms, was in a terrible state for any kind of escape, let alone a scandalous elopement with a young woman! She was bound by these chains forever, and I did not want to hasten our downfall by running away with her. I could never take care of Angelica the way she deserved. We gave each other a beautiful summer, but I knew that everything had to end before we ruined each other's lives."

"And yet, you wrote her a letter saying that you called off the wedding," I say, crossing my arms. "What for? Didn't you realize that it would only cause her more suffering?"

I drain my glass and study Adeline's face, animated by wine and memory. For a moment, I see her past self—a lost eighteen-year-old girl in love with a woman twice her age.

"This letter was a reckless act," she says, "just like my change of heart at the very altar. I caused so much chaos in Angelica's life that she had the right to know I mustered up the courage to change my own, albeit not in the way we wanted. And I felt obligated to write something because she was the one who gave me the wedding dress—it was her parting gift. I brought it to Saint Petersburg. Do you want to take a look?"

"You wanted to return it to her, didn't you?" I ask.

"I wanted to, but I couldn't," Adeline says. "It hurts a lot to bring up the past. I would rather leave everything as it is."

Her words sound sincere, and I begin to see the recklessness in Angelica's actions. Why did a grown woman decide that a girl from a wealthy family would easily leave her pampered and safe life to run away with a Russian aristocrat, knowing nothing about her past? How dare Madam Lissova even hope for it and accuse her of betrayal when Adeline was only a scared child? Perhaps, if Madam Lissova had found the right words, Adeline would have called off the engagement.

"Are you saying that Angelica left your elopement plan as soon as you told her about Raphael?"

"Yes. She called me a traitor and left," Adeline says, wiping her tears with the back of her hand. "You see—I was inexperienced and hoped that she would help me cancel the engagement. Of course, Angelica did not do this. Out of pride or fear, she refused to fight for our feelings and only accused me of betrayal, although I never said I wanted this wedding. She acted very abruptly, and it helped me understand that in the end, I made the right choice. I am not Anna Karenina, and I won't throw myself under a train or risk my future for love. Alas!" Adeline rises from her armchair and walks over to the wardrobe.

"I finally understand," I say, clasping my hands together. Forgive me for all my harsh words." I watch as Adeline opens the wardrobe and runs her hand over the wedding dress, hidden in its gloomy depths, like a ghost from the distant past.

"It's alright," she says, turning around to glance at me. "Ten years ago, I would have said the same thing."

"You think I'm a fool, don't you?" I ask, and my voice trembles, betraying my embarrassment.

"A fool? Not at all. In many ways, your intelligence surpasses mine," Adeline says, and I notice a subtle flush of colour in her cheeks. "I am in awe of the ease with which you mastered teaching the English lectures. It took me many years to perfect this skill, and you are all set in three weeks. Sometimes, your profound knowledge scares me."

"Oh, but I know nothing at all," I say, dropping my eyes to escape her intense gaze.

"You remind me of the twenty-year-old Adeline," she says, "the brilliant girl who had everything ahead of her."

"You are still this girl," I say, looking up at her. "Don't talk like your life is over!"

"That's what those who have just begun their lives always say," she whispers.

I walk up to Adeline, and she freezes, gazing at me through the veil of tears.

"Listen," I say, taking her hand in mine, "I'm not you, and you're not Angelica. We could always find a way to—"

"Margo!" Adeline flinches, raising her voice. "I want to see a future with you, but I can't—not now."

I nod and remain silent.

Not now, I repeat to myself, studying our reflection in the mirror—two women holding hands in the dark, afraid to look at each other.

In the muted glow of the candles, Adeline's living room resembles a magical grotto. Of course, we have no future. Only this moment exists—the fair creature doomed to bathe in one hour of pure pleasure—but isn't this hour what the poets call the most wonderful time of their lives?

"I want to see you wearing this wedding dress," I tell her, running my hand over the white silk and delicate lace of the veil.

"Don't even try to convince me that I am still young and beautiful," Adeline says, smiling. "Prepare yourself for a huge disappointment."

"Please, do it for me." I squeeze her hand tightly. "I swear I won't ask you for anything else."

"What—no more personal questions?" Adeline squints at me. Her eyes glow with mischief.

"I promise," I say, putting my hand over my heart.

"That's a tempting proposition. Then, I'd love to be your one-night bride!" Adeline laughs. I watch as she disappears through the bedroom door, carrying the dress like a newborn child. I sink to the floor in an exhilarating anticipation I've never experienced before.

My head spins, light and airy from the wine. The North Wind wails outside, and the candles reflecting in the darkened mirrors shift and change like the waltzing couples at the Winter

Palace. I feel the contemptuous ladies in Adeline's paintings watching me. They whisper to each other:

Just look: poor Margarita is mad with love! She has completely lost her pride! Silly, silly girl.

I brush them off, listening to the muffled rustle of silk coming from Adeline's bedroom. Finally, a beguiling melody begins to play in the distance. At first, I take it for my imagination, but soon the characteristic crackle of the gramophone tells me it's Adeline's way of distracting me from her brief absence.

I want to press my ear to the door and listen to this strange, mesmerizing melody. When I stand up to come closer, my one-night bride appears.

Clad in a white dress, Adeline holds a silver candelabra in her right hand, dispelling the darkness like a comet leaving a lambent trace on the tenebrous canvas of the starry sky.

"Do you like it?" Adeline puts the candelabra on the chest of drawers and starts spinning. Her veil lifts, and I see the gentle glow of her skin as if the dress has endowed Adeline with dangerous midnight magic.

Unable to speak, I approach her like a moth drawn to the flame.

"I feel the distant echo of falling in love," Adeline says, smiling at me. "That's why I decided to let the sylph dance play. You don't mind, do you, my fair creature?"

Bewitched by the sparkle in her eyes, I want to ask Adeline who the sylphs are and why they are dancing, but I cannot stop looking at her, absorbing her new-found beauty. The light she emits seems too sublime, and I don't want to destroy its magic.

"Love," I say, "and how do you know that you are in love?"

She leans closer to me. One more step, and I will dissolve in the warmth of her penetrating gaze.

"When I can see the soul flickering behind your eyes… that's how I know," she whispers in my ear.

I freeze, trying to hold on to the last bits of my sanity, but an unfathomable force takes over my mind. There is nothing I want more than to fall asleep in this woman's arms tonight.

"If there was a star for every mistake I have made, we would have lived in an endlessly white night," I say. "I don't want to make another mistake. I don't want to lose you."

Adeline's eyes glisten like two iridescent oceans of fire. She does not answer. I cover her hand with mine, noticing the opal ring—the one she wore when I took her to the roof of St. Isaac's Cathedral—a tiny moon rests in my palm, sparkling in the silver January night.

"When you return to Paris, will you remember?" I want to add "me," but the word has too much weight, and I cannot lift it off my tongue.

"I will never forget this evening," Adeline says, still looking into my eyes as though they were stars and she wanted to steal their light.

"Because of the Mariinsky?" I ask. Her closeness makes my skin tingle.

"Because you called me a liar!" Adeline laughs.

"A very beautiful liar," I say, cupping her face with my hand.

"Oh, you cruel, cruel girl!" Adeline's hands clasp around my waist. Her veil brushes against my cheek.

"What is this feeling?" I glance at her, unable to resist any longer.

"What feeling, Margo?" Adeline asks, trailing her fingers down my spine.

"I cannot be the only one who feels it, can I?" My chest rises, almost touching hers.

"Have you ever felt this way before?" She probes my eyes for a hint of doubt.

I pause, remembering Sophia—but even our most ardent nights cannot compare to a moment in Adeline's company.

"Never," I whisper, tracing the silky folds of her dress with my fingertips.

Adeline takes my hand and examines it, too narrow and fragile in comparison to her strong, capable wrist.

"Have I ever told you," she says, intertwining her fingers

with mine, "that you have the most beautiful hands I have ever seen?"

Wave after wave of pleasure descends upon me before I can speak again.

"Another lie, Adeline?" I say, my voice billowing past her ears like a soft wind.

"Calling me a liar is your favourite game now, isn't it?" she says, glaring at me. "Well, how about this: you are insensitive, selfish, disrespectful, and unkind..."Adeline presses my wrist to her lips, planting a kiss after each hurtful word. "You have forgotten your lover, your friends, your country, your family—"

"Adeline… please, stop," I beg her.

"Oh, but you don't want me to," Adeline says, glancing up at me. Her eyes are ablaze with something that looks more like anger than passion. "This is what you have desired from the start, my fair creature." She traces her finger along my collarbones. I forget to breathe.

The lilac rays of the northern dawn endow Adeline's skin with a light purple glow, and I dissolve in her subdued light. She closes her eyes and leans closer. My gaze lingers on her lips, shining under the delicate lace of her veil.

If you do this—you lose her—the North Wind whispers—*and if you don't—you lose everything.*

My lips touch hers—through the veil, through all the

differences between us, through the electrifying gaps left in between our words.

"Not like this." Adeline opens her eyes and lifts her veil, covering us with its snow-glowing lace.

"Is this better?" I say, brushing a loose strand of hair behind her ear.

She wraps her hand around my neck and pulls me closer.

Our lips meet again. Adeline's chest rises under my touch. She consumes every part of my being, inhales the light within me and transforms it into vast, unfathomable darkness.

Stardust cradles me. I no longer exist—not even as a distant thought—I dissipate into nothingness, dreaming in the deep, comforting void. The infamous Lethe has always been there, beaconing to me like a half-sunken lighthouse.

"Wait," I whisper, breaking the kiss to catch my breath.

"It's alright, my fair creature," Adeline says, and the warmth of her voice makes me weak.

I bury my face into the curve of her neck—the familiar scent of crushed roses, violets, and moonlight envelops me. Adeline takes off her veil, letting it brush against my face as it falls.

"Let me help you," she whispers as her fingers run through my hair, caressing every curl.

I feel my dress coming unlaced at the touch of her quick, trembling hands. My breathing becomes heavy, almost forced.

"They say too much love may kill you." Adeline presses her ear to my chest. "Or is it lust?"

A thin layer of my silk chemise separates us. I hear my heart beating louder than it should.

She could have strangled me if she wanted to—a bizarre wine-induced thought pops into my head—*and wouldn't it be better—to die now, in her arms, without having to face the consequences of this night, without having to return home—unwanted, unloved, miserable, and alone?*

"Adeline," I say, breathless, and watch her undress me.

"Don't be afraid." She smiles and helps me up. I step out of the sea-green dress that has fallen at my feet.

"It's already dawn," I say, trying to tear my eyes away from her lips, reddening in the first rays of the sun.

"Are you in a hurry?" Adeline's hands caress my neck, and I reach for the clasp of her gown.

"There's a riot in the city," she says, kissing me again. "Don't leave me. Stay."

"I won't leave you," I say, undressing her.

Blue satin slides off Adeline's sleek shoulders, and, like a black swan, she admires her reflection in my eyes.

Following a wild impulse, I press her body against the wall and let our warmth meld into one.

"No one has ever been so dominant with me," Adeline

gasps. The dress slides off her hips, and I destroy the last barrier left between us.

"I'll make you pay for all the ruined silk," she says, but I don't let her finish, tasting the venom of pleasure on her lips, soft and burning from kisses.

"I will never see you again—never, ever see you again," I say in Russian. My tears fall like warm summer rain on her bare skin.

"Margo, you're scaring me," Adeline replies, her voice hoarse with tension and desire. She frees herself from my embrace.

"You must understand that there is no turning back," she says, looking deep into my eyes.

"I know I am going to lose you," I whisper, "but I don't want to lose this moment, too."

Memorizing her touch, as one takes note of the words inscribed in the sand, I understand that the wave of time will take Adeline away from me soon—it's already dawn, and tomorrow she will leave for Paris.

The pain of imminent loss turns into a sharp blade of feral pleasure. I want to dissolve in Adeline and become a part of her, forgetting the time and space between us. In the cold ocean of her mind, I could create a hearth—a flame that glows in the northern sea—a flame she would never forget.

"Come here." Adeline opens the bedroom door and holds out her hand.

Our fingers intertwine, and my lips, burgundy with wine, find her neck pulsing with passion.

"No matter what happens," Adeline says, "a part of you will always be with me."

"Forever," she repeats, lowering me onto the black velvet bed. "Forever."

I wake up on Adeline's chest. Her steady heartbeat drowns out my disturbing thoughts, and only by looking out the window do I realize that the sun is approaching the horizon again.

"Adeline," I repeat her name like a prayer. "Adeline, my sweet Adeline—take me with you."

She opens her eyes and kisses my forehead.

"You leave me no choice, my fair creature."

"Why?" Bewildered, I gaze at Adeline. Her face emits a ghostly light.

"Pack up, Margo," she says, caressing my hair. "We are going to Paris, after all."

Chapter 8: The Last Passenger

Beneath the burden of her last mistake

MIKHAIL LISSOV'S LETTER TO EUGENE KHOLODOV

January 12

Dearest E,

Be prepared: this letter is going to be as long as your tiresome beard.

Why don't you ever listen to me? You have been very good at hiding all this time, but what you did last night has changed everything. The note I sent was for you to warn Rita about the executioners, not to rush to her apartment and wreak havoc, putting our entire mission at risk. Why couldn't you watch

"Swan Lake" in peace, enjoying the opportunity to spy on Miss Daze?

Now every fool in Saint Petersburg knows we are in charge of the Quiet Resistance! If not for your carelessness, I would not even have to risk writing this, but only one of us can make it and tell the truth. I hope it will be you. In fact, I know it will be you—this time, I am taking all the responsibility. You are just a crazy drunkard following my evil plans, aren't you?

Due to my efforts, the protests are on the rise. Our Empire will lose the war soon, and Greedy Nick's life will be over—you'll see.

My love, you know me—I have never wanted anything more but for us to live in a free country. I regret the blood on my hands, and I don't care what happens to me as long as my friends are safe. We are going to pay for your mistake together, and I'm ready to face its consequences. I will die an honest man, unlike my father.

I am sorry about what I did to Rita—if you live to tell the tale, promise to show her this letter and explain that I never meant what I said at the ball. Maybe she was right. Maybe Miss Daze should not have been our target after all. I am sorry I slapped you, too. I was out of my mind that night, and you were horribly drunk, my dear.

You defended Angelica as if she were an innocent angel—as

if you had never heard her condescending tone or witnessed her pompous "charity" gatherings that bring more drama than donations. I have always cared for you and always will. I care so much that I hate myself for endangering you in every possible way. The revolution has always been an intrusive thought—a way to prove I am better than my father, who had given up without a fight.

I know you wonder where I went after I slapped you and told you not to follow me. I am sorry for breaking your heart in this cruel manner—I needed some time to think. I went to the Neva and walked along the embankment until I reached the port. That is where Rita and I used to spend hours contemplating, dreaming, and discussing poetry. Tell her I remember everything and miss her deeply. She never disappointed me—I disappointed her.

I am losing my train of thought here, and that is because I spent twelve hours out in the cold, not knowing where to go—until my feet carried me to your apartment.

I thought you would be there, waiting for me, trying to sober up after that frightful ball, but your valet gave me a note about Angelica inviting you to the Mariinsky Theatre along with Rita and Miss Daze.

Please, don't deem yourself lucky. Mother always makes these grand gestures for those who praise her the most. I cursed the three of you and went back to the Palace.

Angelica had already left for the theatre, and I had all the time to prepare for the evening protests, but my soul could not rest. I could only think of how my lover and friend betrayed me. I see that you were trying to help, but I succumbed to rage and fear, my dear.

A few hours later, I picked up the evening newspaper. That's how I learned about Novikov's death and the only murder suspect, a woman leaving his apartment, who I thought was Sophia. Who else could it be? At the ball, Rita told me about their affair. Can you imagine how easy it would be for the executioners to attack our girls, considering that Novikov was doing his research for the Emperor himself?

Immediately, I knew Rita was in great danger. I rushed to Moyka Street, hoping to warn her as soon as she returned. It would not have been safe to confront her at the Mariinsky, with my mother and Miss Daze swarming around her like vultures.

Since you went to Rita's apartment right after me, you can imagine what I saw there. When I was approaching the entrance, the executioners crossed the Blue Bridge, their boots still wet with blood. These men cursed like pigs! I hoped it was a coincidence, but my heart knew a horrible thing had happened.

That disgusting old man—Arkady Ivanovich, the hopeless

concierge—do you remember him? When I entered, I noticed his shiny bald head resting on the desk. I thought he was sleeping. Then, I saw a pool of blood on the floor. When I touched him, he was still growling, but his eyes were already glazed over with the white frost of death. The executioners shot him right in the heart. I suppose he did not want to let them in. Who would have thought? This strange little man wanted to protect Rita! Bless his soul.

Now, you can imagine my agitation. I rushed upstairs like a madman. Rita's apartment door was wide open, and the violent draft had already carried a pile of snow into the hall. Someone had emptied all the rooms, and I saw no sign of Sophia.

After reading your note that I opened in haste a few hours ago, I know I should have looked out of the window, as well, but that's history. The only thing of value I found was the music box. I suppose no one paid attention to it since it's so small, and it went right under the bed. I took it with me because I wanted to return it to Rita. I rushed back to the Palace and immediately sent you a messenger with the note.

Then, I attended the protest, hoping that you would keep Rita safe—and you left her in the hands of that haughty Miss Daze! Who knows, maybe this is for the best.

I know you have found shelter, and I trust it's better that we don't meet until tomorrow, but I may not survive until then, so here goes: I gave up Paris completely. I never wanted to leave you, Rita, and Saint Petersburg.

Angelica will survive without me. Worst comes to worst—you will, too. We all have to let go, and I hope to make this as painless as possible. I know you would have preferred me resting in the safety of the Elysian fields in France, but as soon as I saw Rita's butchered apartment, I made up my mind. When Angelica went to the theatre, she left the Nord Express tickets in her study, and I knew what I had to do.

I thought you would come back to the Palace, as I asked you in the note so that you could take my ticket to Rita—she would never take it from me, but, of course, you were too busy saving lives! Angelica returned, scolded me, and said that she was sure Rita had gone away with Miss Daze. I waited until the morning and rushed straight to the Englishwoman's inn.

All of my mother's friends stayed there—this place by the railway station tells you she doesn't want you near for long. Angelica has always been like this: keeping her distance, not letting anyone near her heart. And so I arrived there, told the receptionist who I was, and he went knocking on Miss Daze's door. She appeared like a ghost, distant and aloof—this vulgar woman only had her nightgown on and didn't look too happy to see me.

She was tipsy, too, and had this strange glow in her eyes,

like a hungry accipiter descending on its prey. Her lips and cheeks were burning from lovemaking—in heaven and in hell, I would have recognized this look!

At first, I was enraged and cursed the Englishwoman. I still don't understand that devilish language of hers, but her gestures indicated that Rita was asleep. It was painfully easy to realize what happened between them that night, but I should not care as long as Rita is safe—or so I tell myself.

I made that poor receptionist translate that I wanted her to give Rita my Nord Express ticket along with Sophia's music box. I also asked Miss Daze not to tell Rita I brought them. The Englishwoman kept grinning and nodding. I felt sick looking at her and left without a goodbye.

I hope she takes good care of Rita—for all Miss Daze's theatrical manners and unsolicited advice, I could still see that she has a soul. And Rita does not seem to have a choice now—if she stays even a day longer, the authorities will find her. I tried to explain everything in a way that would not make the receptionist suspicious. I kept repeating, 'this is a life-saving gift for Rita.'

If this doesn't work, I will never forgive myself.

Remember—we are meeting tomorrow. I have what we need to expose the Emperor and make our people rise against him. Do not be late. I am glad mother will be on her way to

Paris soon and will never have to see me face the consequences of my actions.

Rita and Angelica are the only ones worth saving. What you did puts us at risk, so after tomorrow we must part ways forever. I hope this reaches you soon.

Goodbye, Onegin.
Your Lensky

Adeline chuckles at the puzzled look on my face.

"We are going to Paris," I repeat in a sleepy haze. "Do you mean you can take me with you?"

Wrapped in Adeline's robe, I look at her as she stands up and picks something off the dressing table.

"Don't ask me how I got it," she warns before handing me the Nord Express ticket.

"It's for tomorrow!" I gasp. "But this is impossible."

"It's here." She smiles and puts her hands on my shoulders. "We are going to leave Saint Petersburg together, Margo."

Tears fill my eyes, but then I remember Adeline spent the night with me, so she must have gotten the ticket before we arrived at the theatre.

"Why didn't you tell me sooner?"

"I needed to be sure you were prepared to leave everything behind," Adeline says. "That's why I told you my story last night—to show you how difficult it is to make such risky decisions, but I know you are ready now—and we've got no time to lose."

I notice the music box on her nightstand.

"Where did you get this?" I trace my fingers along the familiar gilded lid.

"The maid told me someone left it at the receptionist's desk for you. Still, it's better not to touch old memories before we leave." Adeline packs the music box away into her suitcase.

"Sophia brought it, hasn't she?" I ask, grabbing Adeline's wrist. "Do you know how she found us? Have you seen her?"

Adeline remains silent. Exasperated, I lean on her shoulder.

"Maybe it's for the best," I say. "She let go of me, and I should let her go, too."

"I know it's challenging, but we have to trust each other in order for this plan to work," Adeline says, rubbing my back.

"If I ever had to trust someone with my life, it would have been you," I say. "I know I called you a liar before, but somehow you have remained the most loyal presence in my life. Sophia left, and Misha hates me for not being able to support his cause. Angelica thinks I am a fool. You see, Adeline, I'm a failure in their eyes—but not in yours."

"History will judge them," she says, shaking her head. "It's not your fault this country has wronged you. You should not blame yourself for things that are out of your control and for the actions of people who tried to use you to gain what they needed."

"I understand why Sophia showed up with the music box—after the year we spent together, it is a loving gesture, a genuine attempt to let me know she is trying to forgive and forget, but Misha—why didn't he leave me a note? He could have found me if he wanted to."

"Soon, you'll know who your true friends are," Adeline says, kissing my temples.

"I don't think I have anyone left."

Except for you, I want to add, but the words freeze in my throat.

She tilts my chin up and smiles. "Not even after this night?"

"That was only one night," I whisper.

"Many more to come!" Adeline says, walking over to the wardrobe.

"I have just realized something," I say, watching her pack her dresses, "I have nothing to wear!"

"Don't worry!" She chuckles. "I will find something for you." Adeline picks a black tea gown. "This is the only one that may fit, considering how light you are. Try it on."

I let the dark, heavy fabric sheathe my body, and it awakes me as if I touched the ground after trying to reach the stars.

"What am I going to do in Paris without money and documents? I know some French, but how will I find a job? What if you are making a mistake by taking me with you?" I come up to Adeline and hug her from behind. The sensuous scent of violets still lingers in her tangled hair.

"My fair creature," she says, "I don't want to hurt you with my words, but think of this—do you have a place to return to? Do you have anyone to lean on if you decided to stay? Is it safe after what we have learned about Novikov to even think of returning home?"

"No, but I would rather perish here than become a burden to you. You will begin to hate me for dragging you into this." Tears freeze in my eyes. I bury my head in her shoulder to stop them from seeping through.

"How could anyone hate you?" Adeline hugs me tightly. "I adore you, and I would never let anything bad happen to you. It will only please me to help you find your way. Now, no more pity talk. Help me pack some food and medicine. Our journey will be long and exhausting, especially when the train reaches the war zone."

"Have you seen it?" I ask.

Smoke from explosions, countless dead bodies, fire, and oceans of ash—this is what I imagine when I think of the invasion. I only know what the soldiers—half-mad—have told Sophia, their missing limbs and disordered minds a far more accurate illustration of the war than any existing battlefield.

"If you mean the war," Adeline says, "I haven't seen it, but I observed its consequences. It's everything you can imagine and much, much worse. It is better to lower the blinds when we pass through Ukraine."

"Does the train ever stop there? Could it take refugees on board?"

"Poland sends trains for refugees. No one would board a train leaving the Russian Empire." Adeline empties one of the drawers, and I see her placing diamonds, opals, and emeralds into a wooden box.

"Angelica was right—I am a fool." My voice trembles. "How could anyone consider escaping on a train filled with their worst enemies? And, of course, they would need money to travel. I will be eternally indebted to you, Adeline."

"Don't say such things! Getting you this ticket did not take anything away. It gave me something." She pauses, looking deep into my eyes. "It gave me an opportunity to build the life I always wanted with the person who would never give up on me."

I cup Adeline's face in my hands and kiss her.

"Yesterday, you told me we didn't have a future, and now you are promising to build a life with me," I whisper against her parted lips.

"A wise woman told me I should take more risks." She chuckles, and I see her smile in a way she had never smiled before—this is the hopeful, loving smile of someone who learned to trust again after years of betrayal and lies.

After we pack half of Adeline's wardrobe and order some

food for the long train ride, she sits down at her vanity table.

"Come here, Margo. Let me brush your hair."

I sit in her lap and feel the comb gliding gently against my scalp. I watch the unruly dark-blonde waves straightening under her touch.

"Adeline," I say, listening to the sorrowful cries of the wind in the streets outside, "I will have to pretend to be someone else, won't I? You said Russian inspectors would be checking the train."

"I hope it won't come to that—they care more about those who get into the Capital than those who leave. But you speak perfect English and could pass as my maid. Servants don't require identification."

"So this is who I am from now on—your servant?" I laugh. "That will do."

"Don't be mad at me," Adeline says softly. "You know how much I care about you." She stops brushing my hair and rubs her cheek against mine. "I never thought I would meet someone like you."

I look at our reflection in her mirror and want to freeze this moment in my memory, the way winter blizzards freeze icy patterns on the windows. Our eyes glow softly as the night bathes us in moonlit silks and crowns our heads with stars.

"When I first saw you, my soul recognized yours," I say,

gazing into her eyes. "It was immediate, like lighting a match in the dark and seeing the world for the first time."

"I can only hope this world doesn't disappoint you, my dear," Adeline says, kissing my cheek.

"I still can't believe this is happening—I can't believe I will see Paris with you!" I say, letting her braid my hair while the buzz of excitement sizzles under my skin. "And I am not angry—I am scared. Every time I was so close to achieving something, my dreams vanished without a trace. I have been thinking about Professor Uvarova, too—she needs me at the University, and now—"

"She would understand," Adeline reassures me. "It's only a matter of time before the authorities look into Novikov's death and find your link to his lover. Even if you stayed, you'd be dragged into this investigation that could last for months. But if you don't want to leave Saint Petersburg, I cannot make you."

I turn to look at Adeline. Her eyes sparkle with tears.

"Of course, I want to leave with you!" I say, wrapping my arms around her neck. "Forgive me for being silly. I just wish I could say goodbye to the people I care about."

"I understand," Adeline says, tracing my lips with her thumb, "but we have to be careful, my fair creature."

The maid knocks, and I stand up to open the door. I take a

delicately wrapped box and a note from her trembling hands. She disappears without saying a word.

"Here's our food," I say, and my eyes go wide as I glance at the words on the paper, "and a telegram from Madam Lissova."

"At this hour!" Adeline gasps. "What does she say?"

"She tells you not to worry if she arrives late tomorrow. Something is up with Misha."

"It twists my heart to think how much Angelica suffers because of him. This is exactly why I don't want to have children—or a husband, for that matter. It's just another child to take care of!" Adeline laughs, but I notice an undercurrent of melancholy in her eyes, dark with distress.

"I understand if you would like to visit her," I say, folding the paper between my fingers.

"Angelica can take care of herself," Adeline says, frowning as she cups my face with her hands. "It's you I'm worried about."

"What do you mean?" I shrug, biting my lips.

Adeline drops her voice. "You wouldn't jump off the train if something happened to Misha, would you?"

"What a strange question!" I gaze at her pale, motionless face. "What could happen to him?"

Adeline remains silent. The worry in her eyes seems immeasurable, and I lean in to hug her.

"Adeline, no matter what happens, I will stay with you."

"My fair creature," she says, pulling me in for a kiss, "I want nothing more."

January 13

After hours of packing, Adeline and I join the upper-class crowd waiting for the distant whistle of the Nord Express. Adeline holds my hand as we stand on the platform. I am still wearing her burgundy cloak and the black dress she gave me, as if I had just left someone's funeral to join the city protest. This dark burgundy is the colour of blood freezing in the snow—the first shade of freedom.

Adeline insisted on coming to the station at dawn, two hours before the departure time, and with good reason—the platform overflows with people.

Unlike Adeline, who left most of her decor and clothes as donations to the University, Russian noblemen have brought multiple suitcases, trying to smuggle all their treasures along with them. Panicked and pale, men, women, and children are abandoning their homeland. What makes them run? Is it war, guilt, or uncertainty?

"Are you getting cold?" Adeline asks.

"Not at all," I say. The heat of agitation warms me, and my heart beats faster than the wings of a caged bird attempting to break free.

Adeline wraps her hand around my waist, the sable fur protecting her from the gusts of the North Wind.

Will I see you again? The wind whispers softly. *Are you leaving me forever? How dare you, Margarita? How dare you?*

I don't listen to the wind anymore—its murmur becomes too nonsensical for my exhausted mind.

"So many people are running away!" I say, looking back at the long rows of passengers.

"And some of them want to hop on without a ticket." Adeline smiles, pointing to several groups of young boys waiting in the shadows of the station. "Little do they know, they will get sent straight to the war zone if they try to escape."

"Someone should warn them!" I take a step in their direction, but Adeline holds my hand firmly, unwilling to let go.

"Margo, you have to promise me this: do not stray away from me and do not speak to anyone—do you understand? We must take care of each other because this is all we have left. I know you feel guilty for leaving your loved ones behind, but you cannot save everyone."

I sigh. Of course, she wants to protect me.

"I won't go anywhere—I promise." I squeeze her hand.

Adeline looks around as if she had just committed a crime.

"You may think this is going to be a civilized process," she says, shaking her head. "Well, soon enough, you will see the executioners throwing people off the train, sending them to prison, or worse—"

"Everyone should have the right to escape this horror," I say, looking at the pale, sleepy children clinging to their mothers.

"But not everyone has the means to do so," Adeline says, "and while I wish I could have helped the others, I know I made the right choice." She brushes snowflakes off my hair.

"I hope you won't come to regret it," I say.

We are among the first few in the "upper-class" row, but Adeline keeps turning around to see if someone else has arrived. I know she is looking for Madam Lissova, but it is impossible to find anyone we know in the thick of the crowd.

"She will be alright." I hug Adeline and kiss her cheek, forgetting that we could shock the public with such an intimate gesture. She hugs me back, and her lips linger near my ear.

"It's here," she whispers.

Another gust of the wind brings a long-awaited sound: the train's whistle.

Like a dark-green giant, the Nord Express emerges in the distance, a creamy cloud of smoke crowning the shiny locomotive. The crowd gasps in awe, but Adeline and I stay silent, admiring the life-saving French train as one would greet a long-lost friend. The Nord Express approaches at lightning speed, its metallic wheels rattling and spewing ice from the train tracks.

The train stops with a deafening screech, its wheels glowing like embers in the snow.

A familiar voice reaches my ears. I turn around and see Madam Lissova. Dressed in white fur, with several servants carrying her suitcases, she appears like the Empress herself, gliding past the gaping crowd like a white swan with her head held high. Far behind, Misha follows, his emerald-green coat unbuttoned, revealing a white shirt underneath. I wave, but he does not see me—there are too many people between us.

"They have arrived!" I hold on to Adeline's arm.

"Ah, you have an eagle's eye! I would not have noticed. But we must board the train now." She takes my hand and presents our tickets to the conductor. He barely looks at us and nods, tearing the edge of each ticket.

"There's no going back now," Adeline says, pulling me up the steps of the train.

"We must wait for Misha!" I turn around, trying to distinguish his figure among the hundreds of people boarding the train, but he seems to linger on the steps, searching for his ticket.

I hear Madam Lissova crying, "What's taking you so long?"

"Trust me, they will be fine." Adeline nudges me gently as the porter carries our suitcase into the first-class vestibule.

"I am worried about Misha," I say, tugging at her hand, but Adeline pushes me forward.

"We must go to our compartment now." Her commanding voice makes me submit. I follow Adeline but cannot help turning back, trying to catch another glimpse of Misha. Through the windows, I see people pushing each other, trying to get inside the train. The executioners emerge, just like Adeline said, with their black masks and batons. I can already hear screams piercing the air.

Suddenly, the train whistles, and the floor begins to tremble. I rush back, but it's too late—I feel the strong steel wheels turning under my feet.

"Don't you dare, Margo!" Adeline screams, holding onto my shoulders, but I break free from her grasp and thrust the train door open.

"Misha!" I yell into the distance, and there he is—still standing on the platform, waving goodbye.

"Misha!" repeats another voice, more desolate than mine.

It's Madam Lissova, I think. *How could you do this, Misha? How could you leave us?*

Our eyes meet, and Knyaz Lissov winks at me through his

shiny glasses. He smiles and presses his hand to his lips.

The North Wind carries his words to me.

Stay safe, Rita! Stay safe!

The speeding train carries me away before I can wave or scream. Someone's hands clasp around my waist and pull me back inside.

"What are you doing?" Adeline scolds me. "You could fall!"

"It's Misha." I clench my teeth to hold back the tears. "He stayed. He didn't board the train. Is this why you asked me about him? Did you know?"

"Oh, my fair creature! With Angelica's note, I felt it coming." Adeline presses me to her chest. "What can I say? He made his choice."

"We need to check up on Angelica—we have to do something," I whisper, trembling in Adeline's embrace. Still trying to catch my breath, I let her strong arms cradle me.

"She needs to be alone for now—let her grieve. Misha let you go. Now, let him go, too."

"I am tired of letting people go and losing everyone I love, Adeline. You should have seen the way Misha looked at me—he did not hate me! It was almost like he knew everything—as if he had forgiven me."

"That's because there was nothing to forgive." Adeline kisses my forehead and leads me back to our compartment.

With tears in my eyes, I take Sophia's music box out of the suitcase.

"Don't be shy. Open it," Adeline says. "You are not leaving home. You are bringing it to Paris."

I force a smile, but it dissipates as soon as I see the crumpled note hidden behind the music box's lid. My fingers tremble as I unfold it. I gasp, seeing the familiar handwriting. The note falls from my hands.

"What is this, Margo?" Adeline asks. Her voice echoes in my head like a distant siren.

I freeze and stare at her blankly.

"Sophia," I whisper. "It's her suicide note."

Chapter 9:
Into the Unknown

May a luxuriant, wild garden grow
Where was the land of misery and snow.
January 14

I wrap up my story. The sun emerges from the horizon, bathing the snowy steppe in its crimson light. We must be approaching the war zone. I see smoke in the distance—its grey, feathery wings spread across the sky.

"Now you know everything, Adeline."

"You have begun your tale at midnight and ended at dawn," she says, and her eyes fill with wonder. "How marvellous! You could write a novel about your life."

"Write it for me," I say, shaking my head. "I survived it, and that's enough. I still don't understand why you wanted to know everything, but you have saved me and my future—at least, I owe you that."

"You don't owe me anything, my fair creature. I want to keep you safe." Adeline reaches across the table and touches my wrist. "No one deserves the hardships you've been through. Your story has reminded me that everything happens for a reason, and we have found each other at the right time."

"Be it right or wrong, I cannot believe Sophia is gone." I say, burying my face in my hands. "I am the only person who could have saved her! I even had a vision about her death. What if it could have been prevented?"

"Her final note breaks my heart, too," Adeline says, lowering her voice, "but you must remember that nothing and no one is eternal."

"Death is eternal—but how would you understand?" I clench my fists. "You never lost anyone because you always leave first."

"We've had this conversation before, haven't we?" Adeline gazes at me calmly, and I turn to the window, blinking away the tears.

The ever-changing landscape becomes darker, overshadowed by the tall pine forest. I close my eyes. Adeline sits down next to me and covers my shoulders with her lilac shawl.

"Death is a blessing in disguise," she whispers in my ear, "and grief is the real curse that will haunt you until you learn to accept your mistakes and live with them."

"And what if I can't live with my mistakes?" I whisper back. "What then?"

"In time, you will learn that everything comes full circle." Adeline runs her fingers through my tangled hair. "You have to love someone deeply to let them go, and I trust that you loved Sophia enough to let her spirit rest in peace."

"I don't believe in spirits, and I don't believe in letting go. When you care about someone, you stay with them—until the end." I cannot hold back the tears and sob, resting my head on Adeline's shoulder.

"You have been through so much, my fair creature. It twists my heart to see you like this." She takes a loaf of bread from our suitcase. "Here, have a bite."

I break the loaf in half, and the crunch of its golden crust reminds me—this is my last taste of home.

"I'm going to miss it," I say.

"Russia?"

"The bread." I laugh through the tears. "I'm sure Parisian baguettes aren't bad, but I doubt they can compare to this." I give Adeline the other half, and she smiles, watching me devour my portion.

"I do not share your passion for bread," she says, "you can have it all to yourself. However, I have a better idea: I will ask if the first-class dining car offers tea before lunch."

Adeline disappears behind the sliding doors, and I turn to watch the icy landscape stretching for many miles outside the window. God knows how long it will take us to get to Paris, but at least I am not alone—not anymore.

Someone knocks, waking me from my daydream. Startled, I stand up and listen.

"Adeline! We need to talk."

It's Madam Lissova. I slide the door open, and her eyes meet mine with utter shock.

"Margarita? How did you—"

She pauses, studying my face, and I lower my gaze.

"Ah"—she exhales—"you didn't listen to my advice. Adeline took you with her, didn't she?" Lissova shakes her head.

"I am sorry about Misha," I say, moving over to let her in.

"Don't speak of him ever again." Her voice trembles, and I see waves of pain washing over her glacial grey eyes. The silver in her regal updo shines dimly in the morning light. Her dark purple dress makes Madam Lissova look old and frail—the pale ghost left of the woman who shone so brightly at the Winter Ball.

Following a strange impulse, I hug Madam Lissova. Her cold, stern body melts in my arms. She clasps her hands behind my back.

"He's gone," she murmurs, "gone, gone forever." Desolate sobs rack her body like a boat caught between the waves. I pull Madam Lissova down onto the seat beside me.

"He can't be gone forever—Misha will find his way back to you," I say, knowing it's a lie.

"He is too stubborn, too immature to see the consequences of his actions." Madam Lissova weeps into my shoulder. Her tear-streaked cheeks glow softly when she lifts her head to look at me. "You were his only friend! Didn't he tell you?"

"We haven't spoken since the Winter Ball," I say. "Misha said he was leaving Saint Petersburg with you."

"Oh, this wretched country! It will kill my boy, Margarita. I wanted to protect him, to be a good mother, and even then—I didn't wait for him to board the train. Any mother would have waited, and I—"

"It's not your fault, Madam Lissova."

"Please," she says, cupping my face in her hands—"oh, please, call me Angelica. Don't you understand? You are the last thread that connects me to him… my dear Misha, my only child! I saw him on the platform waving me goodbye and tried to jump off, but the guards—they didn't let me, and—"

"He will be alright," I lie again, trying not to look at her.

"I could never protect him," she says, "and now… now, I only have you."

Angelica weeps and kisses my forehead.

"And Adeline," I add, squinting at the touch of her ice-cold lips on my skin.

"She kept feeding you lies, didn't she? Is this why you stayed?" Angelica hugs me again. "My poor child!"

"She saved my life," I whisper, "she gave me freedom, Angelica—the freedom I could never even dream of." My eyes gleam with passion, and I want to tell her how wrong she was and how much Adeline has changed. "You know, she still keeps the wedding dress you gave her."

"Does she?" Angelica's eyes wander. She looks over my shoulder at the gloomy forests and fields—our great heritage—abandoned, untrodden, unknown, much like our souls, colliding for a brief moment only to drift apart forever.

"She told me how much it means to her—how much you mean to her. You are not alone, Angelica," I repeat.

She becomes smaller and weaker in my arms as if some great force of nature has taken all her power and grace, burying it in the northern snow.

"It never snows in Paris," Angelica says, "and if it does—the snow melts before it touches the ground. I wanted to show it to Misha—winter without snow. He is alone now. He doesn't have anything left—no money and no home. I took everything when I left. I must get back to him as soon as possible."

"Angelica, you must be strong," I say, taking her hand in mine. "Misha wanted you to get on this train. He wanted to protect you."

"Oh, I wanted to be strong, but I can't anymore. I will get off at the next stop."

"No, you won't!" Adeline's voice startles us. She returns with the tea tray, and the intoxicating aroma of bergamot fills the air. "My dear Angelica, the next stop is the war zone. We are past the point of no return."

"Adeline," Madam Lissova stutters, looking at the tray with three cups of tea, "how did you know I was here?"

"I went to your compartment, but you weren't there, so I made a guess," Adeline says. "Please, have some tea and promise us not to escape."

"Where could I possibly go?" Angelica smiles bitterly, taking the teacup in her hands. "Into the unknown?"

For a moment, everyone falls silent, and the clink of our teaspoons merges with the steady rattle of train wheels.

"We are travelling through strange lands," Angelica says, gazing out of the window, where the snow-powdered hills grow taller and taller, submerging us in the kingdom of ice. "I do not recognize this scenery at all."

"All landscapes are the same in Russia: snow, ice, pine forests, and desolation," Adeline says, putting her hand on

Angelica's shoulder. "And you are in great distress—you have just lost your son."

"Misha knows how to take care of himself," I interfere, trying to shield Angelica from Adeline's bluntness.

"My son will die in front of the Winter Palace, Margarita. It's over," Angelica says, lowering her voice. "Last night, he told me everything. I haven't been able to eat or sleep since then." She takes a sip of tea and winces.

"My poor darling, what did he tell you?" Adeline leans closer and takes her hand.

"It's Misha—he led the Quiet Resistance," Angelica says, holding back the tears. "He is going to sacrifice himself for this pointless movement."

"The Quiet Resistance," Adeline whispers, "I missed a lot, haven't I?"

"Let's not talk here." Angelica shakes her head. "Their ears are everywhere. I will meet you at lunch." She rises, preparing to leave.

"At least finish the tea, my dear!" Adeline stands up, still holding her hand.

"I don't feel well—forgive me." Angelica slides the door open and turns around to look at me. Her gaze lingers on my black dress. "The truth is, I always preferred to suffer alone," she says in a thin, breaking voice.

"What nonsense you talk! You shouldn't be alone. I will escort you to your room." Adeline wraps her hand around Angelica's waist, and the door shuts behind them.

"You have lost your mind!" I hear Angelica's whisper. "What are you going to do with her?"

"With Margo, you mean? What *wouldn't* I do with her?" Adeline laughs.

"It was you," Angelica hisses, "driving wedges between her and my son, and look where he is now!"

"You are blaming the wrong woman, my dear." Adeline's sinister reply freezes me to the bone. "Like any child, Misha wanted love, which you could not give him, always distracted by your parties and vanity—"

I hear a sharp slap followed by Angelica's receding footsteps.

Adeline returns with a crimson mark burning on her cheek.

"Ah, the joys of first-class travelling!" she says. "You never know what happens next!"

"You did not have to be this cruel. Angelica is in pain—can't you see that?" I press my hand to her burning cheek.

"You cannot simply drag someone into the life they didn't choose," Adeline says, pushing my hand away. "If Angelica respected her son's wishes, she wouldn't have to feel this pain."

"She is a mother," I say, bitterness making my hands turn

to fists. "Mothers want to keep their children safe—it's an instinct stronger than forces of nature. And why did you lie to her—about not knowing what the Quiet Resistance was when I told you everything hours ago?"

"Their ears are everywhere," Adeline echoes Angelica's words, "and safety is an illusion."

"But I feel safe here, with you," I say.

Adeline looks away, and her eyes cloud with regret.

"One moment, you fall asleep in your lover's arms," she says, "and the next—you are alone, battling with the never-ending storm. But let's not think about Angelica, or Misha, or Sophia." Adeline notices my cup, still brimming with tea. "Why don't you finish your tea? Drink it, and I will tell you a story."

I surrender—there is no use in fighting now.

"Thank you for taking care of me," I say, my voice softened by fatigue. "You have been incredibly kind all this time, and I never mentioned how grateful I am to share this journey with you."

"It's a pleasure to take care of you, my fair creature. You deserve all the kindness in the world," Adeline says. Her tea cools down while she looks out to the hoarfrost-covered spruce forest, with each tree wearing a heavy armour of snow and ice on its needles.

I drink until the cup is drained. A strange, overpowering

dizziness envelops me like a fog.

"I feel like falling asleep all of a sudden," I say, yawning.

"Come here, my fair creature—you don't have to sleep over there." Adeline pushes the tray away and lets me lie down. I bury my face in her lap.

"What was the story you wanted to tell me?" I whisper, inhaling the familiar scent of her perfume.

"Oh, you'll enjoy this one. It's similar to yours, but more… tragic." Adeline laughs, stroking my hair, lulling me to sleep with every motion of her opal-ringed hand.

"How could anything be more tragic?" I look up at Adeline, studying the tiny creases appearing at the corners of her eyes when she smiles.

"Soon, you will submerge into a deep, oblivious slumber. The time has come for me to tell you everything," she says, intertwining her fingers with mine.

My heart sinks into a dark, bottomless void. I realize I can no longer move. Paralyzed, I attempt to speak, but the words get stuck in my throat as the chains of horror shackle my body.

"Don't worry—my poison won't kill you—it will only prevent you from escaping your fate," Adeline whispers. "It's a small dose of the deadly nightshade. I put it in your tea. It isn't strong enough to stop your heart."

I squirm in her arms, unable to make a sound.

Adeline presses her ear to my chest and laughs. "Oh, how fast it's beating! What sweet music it makes—"

"How could you," I can barely squeeze out the words, "how could you do this to me? And Angelica—"

"Yes. Angelica, too," she says with a blood-chilling smile. "Are you afraid?"

Adeline's voice rings in my ears like an echo in the desert. I realize that something has changed. She is speaking in Russian now—pure, well-versed Russian, with only a slight hint of the British accent. Terrified, I want to scream, but nothing comes out of my mouth, sealed with her brief, fleeting kiss.

"Sometimes, we hurt those we care about without wanting to," Adeline continues, her lips brushing against my ear. "Perhaps, at another time, under other circumstances, things would have been different, but I had to get all the information I needed."

"You did not even need a translator! I knew you were a liar," I hiss, and my body shudders with pain. "Oh, why did I ever believe you?" I try to wrench free from her grip, but Adeline's strong arms hold me down like the claws of a hawk carrying its prey.

"You believed me because you were vulnerable," she says. "It was painfully easy to lure you in—I only gave you the protection and understanding that your soul craved, and you were mine. I did not lie when I said I came to Saint Petersburg for you."

"Who sent you then?" I say through the veil of heavy fog blurring my senses as the poison enters my blood.

Adeline's dark eyes float above me, her gaze as piercing and passionate as it was last night when I fell asleep in her arms.

"The British Empire's Committee of Imperial Defence has ordered me to investigate the revolutionary activities in Saint Petersburg," she says, grinning at my agony. "Mikhail Lissov possessed valuable information that I could only get through his closest friend—you, Margo." Adeline pauses to wipe my burning forehead with her handkerchief.

"And why does your government care about our revolution?" I whisper, fighting the darkness that entangles my mind.

"Revolutions are a threat to all Empires. It's my job to prevent them," Adeline says. Her eyes shine with pride.

"Look at all the lives you have ruined for a scrap of information—"

"Brace yourself, my dear," she interrupts me with a grin. "Soon you will hear about Mikhail's shameful death as the traitor to the Motherland. Don't blame yourself—you couldn't have known that I recorded everything you said. I take great pride in doing my job impeccably well."

My heart shudders in pain, but I can only gaze up at

Adeline, her face pale and serene, like the blessed image of a martyr with a radiant halo above her head.

"Before taking her life, Sophia played a major role in my mission, as well," she says, tapping on the lid of my music box. "I told you that Misha stole her diary at Angelica's ball—well, that was me."

I growl through the tears, wanting to crush the hands that still caress me.

"Ah, you are adorable when you struggle, but don't get angry." Adeline laughs at the tears rolling down my cheeks. "I had to frame him—otherwise, you would not have given yourself to me so willingly."

I close my eyes, hoping this nightmare is just another hallucination—a waking dream—but when I open them, Adeline still holds me in her tight grip and smiles ruthlessly, enjoying my pain.

"Do you remember the glass of champagne I gave you before Angelica's toast?" she asks, wiping my tears with her thumb. "I laced your drink and went through your purse when you passed out. Poor Misha—he was so worried about you, but you acted like a silly, gullible girl, falling right into my meticulous trap, giving me everything I needed—and so much more." Adeline runs her fingers through my hair and smiles when I flinch.

"After I returned you home to Sophia, I paid Novikov a brief visit, pretending to be the grieving wife of his deceased patient," she continues, winding my curls on her slender finger. "The black dress I wore at the ball made quite an impression—Novikov let me in, offered his solace and a glass of vodka. Then, I killed him." Adeline laughs.

"You couldn't," I murmur, looking into the dark pits of her merciless eyes.

"Oh yes, I could," she says, pulling my hair until I squeal in pain. "Poisoning him was a pleasure like no other! Wherever I go, I always carry some belladonna—the femme fatale of the forest—an untraceable poison that mimics a heart attack. Using my charm and a tiny distraction, I spilled death into his glass. It always surprises me how your doctors drink vodka, saying it's good for the soul when it can stop their heart just as easily as the tincture of a mandrake root."

"You are a monster," I wheeze. Her cold, dispassionate smile makes me shiver.

"Ah, darling, you give me too much credit," Adeline says, releasing my hair from her deft fingers. "With the dangerous work Novikov had been doing, torturing the soldiers with his questionable therapy, he would have died one way or another—I only helped him go to Hell in peace."

I feel the blood rushing to my heart. It beats faster and faster with every word she says.

"While he was convulsing on the floor, ridiculous and helpless," Adeline continues, "I had unearthed more evidence of your revolutionary plans than I ever hoped to find. Novikov did not gather information about you for the Emperor. Your beautiful mind fascinated him, and he wanted to understand what triggers your hallucinations. Don't worry—I stole most of his research, so you will never know what he discovered."

"You killed Sophia, too," I whisper. Adeline presses her finger to my quivering lips.

"Oh, cruel as I am, you are the one responsible for her death. I knew she would run straight to Novikov after seeing you in my arms. Your carelessness pushed her into oblivion. I left some of the evidence on purpose—I had no doubt she would burn it, adding to the list of her crimes. You can say anything you want about Sophia, but she was loyal to you until the very end. I framed her as the main suspect in Novikov's murder, and she had smartly chosen suicide over life in prison—but that would never happen if you had not danced with me at the Winter Ball."

Adeline takes Sophia's note and tears it apart. "Poor lost soul! May she rest in peace!"

I try to protest, but only a feeble moan escapes my mouth.

"Oh, I will never forget the way you trusted me. I already

miss your innocence," Adeline muses. "As for last night… I played a role because I wanted to make you happy, knowing how many trials await you. You have to understand that I was just doing my job. With or without me, your fate was sealed. Trust me: in the place you've been sent to, you'll need these precious memories of all the happy times we shared."

Adeline wraps her arm around my neck. I struggle for air.

"Ah—one last thing!" she says, gazing deep into my eyes. "I gave you Misha's ticket. I wanted to hand you over to the authorities, but this impertinent young man chose your safety over his life, so I had to change my plan not to raise suspicion. Now, you are responsible for his death, too, my dear. It's a pity Misha didn't know this train's actual destination—otherwise, he wouldn't let you board it."

"What destination?" I dig my nails into her skin.

"Oh, you'll recognize this place soon enough," Adeline says with bloodcurdling tenderness. "Remember: life punishes us not for our complicity, but for our shame. You carry too much guilt on your shoulders, and you would have drowned in it sooner or later. Consider this exile my parting gift to you and Angelica."

"How could you, Adeline? How could you make me believe something that was never true?" I whisper, struggling to keep my eyes open.

"Maybe it *was* true—but only for a moment. Remember how I told you that I lost something, too? In times like these, we do not have a choice." Adeline looks down at me with the same warmth and compassion I saw in her gaze when we danced at the Winter Ball. Tears stream down my cheeks, and she wipes them away, kissing me one last time.

"Sleep now, my fair creature."

Unable to fight any longer, my consciousness dissolves into the all-encompassing darkness.

In this blind, impenetrable night, I can still see the faint glimmer of a scintillating future that no longer belongs to me—all my wishes and dreams dissipating like morning stars. Was it all for nothing?

Adeline's hands caress me through this dreadful slumber. She is singing a lullaby, and I cling to her voice, but its melody becomes softer and softer until I cannot hear it at all. Every heartbeat takes me away from her—the woman who betrayed my trust—the woman I should hate but still admire.

Epilogue

A soft cover of silvery evening fog caresses Saint Petersburg's endless spires crowned by angels and stars.

Knyaz Lissov returns from the train station. Rushing to Saint Isaac's Cathedral, he recalls the bitter farewell with Rita and Angelica.

Could she hear me? Does she know I wished her well? Misha thinks, picturing Rita's face, pale with sorrow and shock. Angelica's screams echo in his mind like the distant chimes of cathedral bells.

Don't grieve for me, mother. Don't grieve for me.

Misha climbs the familiar staircase to Saint Isaac's rooftop. He showed Rita this hidden path years ago when they had just met. She observed the icy panorama of the sleeping city, and he marvelled at the childlike awe in her eyes.

"Misha, you crazy boy! Don't fall!" Rita screamed, seeing him jump onto the colonnade's granite edge. Misha lifted her up, and, a moment later, they stood next to each other, facing the glimmering Saint Petersburg, its snow-powdered streets woven with fairy tales and dreams.

"Now you have to stretch your arms out like this," he told her, pointing at the half-frozen wings of the bronze angel standing next to them.

"Are we going to jump?" Rita said, laughing as the wind lifted her arms.

"No," Misha turned to face her. "We are going to fly! Now or never!"

Faster than Rita could answer, he lifted her and glided over the edge of the colonnade, from one angel to another, with the blizzard singing in his ears.

"One day, you will kill us both!" Rita yelled and laughed, lighting a flicker of joy in the still northern night.

Although I will never hear her voice again, I am happy for Rita—she is better off with Miss Daze in Paris than here, with me, Misha thinks, woken from his daydream by the distant gunfire. The revolution is near.

He spurs onward, shaking snowflakes from his unruly hair.

Eugene waits for him on the roof. Kholodov's brown fur coat and ushanka make him look like a bear that came out of the deep Siberian forest.

"Well done!" Misha says, waving at Kholodov, "I almost

didn't recognize you."

"Shhh," Eugene hisses, looking around. "Aren't we meeting in secret?"

"Only fools have secrets—wise men sin openly." Misha smirks, admiring the frozen landscape and the terracotta flames of the setting sun on the Winter Palace's windows.

"I thought I would never see you again," Eugene says, holding his hands out for a hug.

Misha plunges into his arms, and they embrace as the North Wind whistles around them.

"This is the last time," Knyaz Lissov whispers. "But you never thought we'd last anyway, did you?"

Tears run down Eugene's bristled cheeks.

"Have you seen Rita? Is she safe?" he asks, burying his head in Misha's shoulder.

"The Nord Express has just departed," Misha says, "she was there—I saw her with Miss Daze."

"Good. Has Angelica tried to stop you?"

"She did, but the guards did not let her jump off the train." Misha shakes his head. Even a simple attempt to picture his mother's agony breaks his heart.

"I cannot imagine your pain," Eugene says, caressing his lover's hair. "Let's hope it will be over soon."

"I have brought everything you asked for." Misha takes an

envelope from his pocket and hands it to Eugene. "These are Dr. Novikov's patient files. They will help us overthrow the Emperor," he announces with flames of rage burning in his eyes.

"But what's next?" Eugene says, hiding the envelope in the folds of his fur coat. "Where will you go, my love? Must we really part?"

"Yes. And you must forget me." Misha's voice trembles, weak against the deafening wind.

"I won't forget." Eugene wipes his tears with the edge of Misha's emerald coat. "And how could I ever forget someone who turned me into the enemy of the Motherland?"

"You always have to ruin the moment," Misha says, laughing, but sorrow glimmers in his gaze. "I am the enemy here—you're only a pawn in my skilled hands."

Eugene studies the familiar soft glow of Knyaz Lissov's grey eyes bedimmed with tears.

"It seems like only yesterday you came to my lab, whispering about freedom, telling me we are the force this country needed, and now—" Eugene stutters, wincing in pain.

"You aren't going to make me cry, Kholodov. I'm allergic to feelings, remember?" Misha growls, taking off his glasses.

"You had me wrapped around your finger, Misha—and I will never regret it." Eugene traces his thumb over his lover's lips, chapped from the cold.

"We can't. Not anymore." Lissov pushes his hand away.

With Misha's soft curls brushing against his cheek, Eugene asks, "Are they watching us?"

"They are always watching—and you better go," his lover whispers, breaking free from the embrace. "We should end this."

"Farewell, my dear," Eugene says, taking a step back. "I owe you my sanity in this profoundly insane world. May we see each other at a more peaceful time!"

Four executioners emerge from behind the statues of St. Isaac's angels. Eugene turns around, facing their sparkling black guns. A deep, raucous voice emerges from the void of their motionless masked faces.

"Knyaz Mikhail Lissov, the Imperial Court has charged you with national treason. For this unpardonable crime, the Emperor has sentenced you to death."

"Eugene," Misha whispers, "you better close your eyes."

Kholodov attempts to shield him, but Misha stops Eugene with a wave of his hand.

"I will die a decent death," he says, and Eugene drops to his knees, watching the executioners surround Misha as he stands on the edge of the colonnade. The wind winnows his hair, shining like gold in the last rays of the sun.

One of the executioners steps forward. "Knyaz Lissov, you have the right to say your last words before we carry out your sentence," the voice behind the black mask proclaims.

"How generous of you, gentlemen!" Misha grins, unbuttoning his shirt. "My final word is simple: Russia will be free. Free from corruption. Free from war. Free from your bloody Emperor! Now, kill me, cowards!" He points at his chest. "You can stop my heart, but you won't stop the revolution."

Misha spreads his arms, imagining Rita standing next to him. *She would not have flinched. She would have remained brave. Braver than me,* he thinks. For a moment, Misha can almost feel her hand touching his shoulder.

"Now or never," he whispers.

The executioners pull their triggers.

Two seagulls fly off the cathedral's roof at the sound of gunshots, and the world turns silent, eclipsed by the shadow of death.

Hit by four bullets, Misha stumbles and falls, raising his arms to the vast scarlet sky. A faint smile lingers on his lips.

I am flying, he thinks. *Finally, I have tasted freedom.*

"Misha!" With a shrill, desolate cry, Eugene rushes to the edge of the colonnade and sees his lifeless body in the blood-drenched snow. Misha's hands, still reaching for something, rest on the icy cobblestone pavement. Crimson flowers bloom on his chest, tarnishing the white silk of his unbuttoned shirt. Misha opens his mouth in a final exhale.

How free it is—you have no idea how free, he thinks, looking up at the distant face of his lover.

If only I could show this to Rita! Oh, Death, how warm you are, how kind and forgiving! Misha smiles, and the North Wind lifts him—up, up, and away until he becomes one with the orange haze of the setting sun.

Eugene freezes with shock, and his nails scratch the cold marble in vain. The colonnade's guardian angels lower their heads in prayer. He watches as sorrow and regret wash over their stone faces, darkened by grief.

"Why couldn't you protect him?" he whispers. "Oh god, why couldn't you save the only soul I ever loved!"

Eugene hears the heavy clatter of the executioner's boots approaching him from behind. Instinctively, he reaches for the envelope hidden in his fur coat.

"Thank you for your service." The executioner takes Novikov's papers from Eugene's trembling hands and pats him on the shoulder. "The Emperor needs more people like you."

January 14

An abrupt stop wakes Margarita. She finds herself alone in the empty train compartment. Everything is gone except for the burgundy cape that Adeline draped over her unconscious body before leaving.

Margarita's memory returns bit by bit. She remembers the cold overcrowded station, Angelica's tears, Adeline's ominous smile, and the fatal belladonna hidden in her opal ring.

Farewell, my fair creature.

Margarita jumps up in horror.

"Let me out!" she screams, trying to open the door.

A prison guard's emotionless voice greets her from the other side.

"Margarita Gradova, in Emperor's name, you have been sentenced to ten years in katorga for spreading anti-imperial ideas among the students of Saint Petersburg Imperial State University. You have the right to remain silent."

Ten years! Margarita thinks. *Ten years of imprisonment for talking about freedom!*

"This must be a mistake! Please, let me out!" she begs, but no one answers her cries. She circles the compartment, hands tugging at her tangled hair.

"This must be a dream," she whispers, looking out the frozen window.

A ghost-like woman in a diaphanous white dress stands on the platform of an unfamiliar station. Margarita recognizes her veiled face, softer than velvet and paler than snow. Their eyes meet, and the intensity of the woman's dark gaze draws her in, devouring the remnants of sanity in her tortured soul.

"Adeline," Margarita whispers, pressing her hand against the icy glass.

Another train flashes through the station, and the vision is gone—the ghost disappears, carried away by the wind.

Margarita feels a sudden jolt. The wheels start turning with a long, heart-wrenching howl, and she realizes that her train is going east—back to Siberia.

- THE END OF TRANSCRIPTION -

February 21, 1905
Paris, France

To the Committee of Imperial Defence:

As requested, I am sending you the complete transcription of my conversations with M.G., along with the letters and diary entries integral to the investigation. I have copied and attached them to preserve the chronological order of events.

Always at your service,
- A.D.

Adeline finishes writing her letter and stands up from the antique mahogany desk.

"It's done," she concludes, tracing her fingers over the last page of the manuscript. As always, she hasn't missed a thing.

Stretching her arms with a sigh of relief, Adeline reaches for the bottle of Chardonnay resting on the marble mantelpiece. When the clock strikes midnight, she raises her glass.

The wind howls outside, and Adeline looks out the window, inhaling the crispy freshness of the winter night. Hypnotized by the magnificent view of the Eiffel Tower glimmering in the moonlight, she ties the lilac shawl around her shoulders.

After all the weeks spent in the cold, hostile Saint Petersburg, Adeline expected to miss the freeing French air. Instead, she misses the distant chime of St. Isaac's Cathedral and the patterned ice of the Neva River.

"How unprofessional," she whispers, "to think I have become a sentimental thief!"

Adeline winds up Margarita's music box and closes her eyes, dissolving in the dreamy melody. She recalls it all like a distant dream—the way she remembers all her missions—but something is different about this one.

What is it? she thinks, tilting her head to the rhythm of the waltz. An unfamiliar pang of guilt tugs at her heart.

The melody breaks in the middle and fades away, like a half-told story waiting to be continued.

"Don't be angry, Margo," Adeline whispers, "Remember—nothing is eternal, least of all this wretched winter."

As if refuting her words, a strong gust of wind swings the window open, and the pages of Adeline's manuscript fly apart, whirling like snowflakes in the blizzard. She curses, catching a few of them seconds before they disappear in the fiery jaws of her fireplace.

Adeline slams the window, but the otherworldly song rings in her ears like an ancient prayer.

I will return, whispers the North Wind. *I will always return.*

Acknowledgments

Dear readers, you have all my gratitude for joining Margarita on her journey. I hope you realize this is not the end—the North Wind will return with the next part of her story.

I thank Guy Allen for making this book possible: without his ongoing guidance and support, *The Dawn of Eternal Winter* would have remained a faint idea at the back of my mind. Every writer, no matter if they are starting out or publishing their tenth novel, needs someone who believes in them, and he was this person for me.

I am grateful to my editor, Ola Pokolenczuk, for her hard work and compassion. She was taken with my story from the start and dedicated many hours to developing my manuscript into a refined work. I presented her with a challenging task, and she took this opportunity to offer helpful feedback and polish my writing voice.

I also thank Kristina Maltseva for the brilliant cover design that captures Margarita's spirit. It has always been my dream to see St. Isaac's Cathedral at dawn on the cover. I am grateful to Kristina for her artistic passion and enthusiasm that made my ideas shine.

Laurel Waterman's course "Editing: Principles and Practice" has changed my entire approach to writing and revision. By working with other writers and editors, I have learned that the creative process requires a supportive community and a wise mentor. I cannot thank Laurel enough for all the hard work she did to help me become the writer I am today.

Dr. Kate Holland and her research project "Digital Dostoevsky" inspired me in many ways. I spent the summer of 2022 encoding Fyodor Dostoevsky's novel *The Adolescent* using XML and TEI, and this experience gave me the precision I needed to perfect my own work. I also thank Dr. Holland for seeing the beauty of Russian literature and culture even after the horrifying invasion of Ukraine started by Russia on February 24, 2022.

In the dark months following the invasion, when I wanted to erase every part of my Russian heritage, Dr. Holland and her project helped me understand the importance of writing from the perspective of my heroine. This is how Margarita became the eye of the storm—someone who can observe the chaos of an authoritarian regime from within and talk about it openly at the time of great distress.

Quinn, Kristine, and Malou—thank you for your friendship, kindness, generosity, and support that allowed me to complete this manuscript. Even when I had to isolate myself from the world, you remained my beacons of light and hope.

Mom and Dad, even though we are oceans apart, I could feel your presence as I wrote. I promise to translate this work for you once it is safe to publish back home.

Dear Grandma, you passed away in February 2023, and your spirit guided me as I prepared this manuscript for publication. Your kindness and wisdom are my light on the darkest nights. Thank you for your unconditional love and support. I will always cherish your memory.

About the Author

Veronika Sizova is a bilingual writer born in Yekaterinburg, Russia. Her writing career began in 2016 with the publication of her poetry and short stories collection *Дверь в Вечность (The Door to Eternity)* in Russian.

In 2021, Veronika moved to Canada to study English and Professional Writing & Communication at the University of Toronto. Her plans include working in the field of digital humanities and continuing the path of a novelist with the sequel to her debut novel set for release in 2024.

You can find a portfolio of Veronika's creative work (poetry, short stories, literary and film criticism) in Russian and English at her website, *The Waves of Poetry (www.thewavesofpoetry.com).*

Manufactured by Amazon.ca
Bolton, ON

33969002R00146